Losing You (Prequel to It's Not Over). Copyright© 2014 by Melissa M Marlow. All rights reserved. Printed in the United States of America. For information address Poehler Publishing, Ramsey Minnesota. Book design provided by Melissa Poehler with Poehler Publishing.

Co Editor: Kevin McNally

Photos from 123RF

www.mmmarlow.com

ISBN-13: 978-0-9835245-4-0

Ebook-13: 978-0-9835245-5-7

First Edition: September 2014

# Losing You

## Prequel to It's Not Over

By

### Melissa M Marlow

Poehler Publishing

# *Contents*

## Contents

# Preface

## Paul

As a man, sex is important to us as a group. We want it, desire it, and will beg for it, if we have to, but love completes you by filling your heart with happiness. I wanted Jessica Jenson to be mine and only mine. It's a nightmare thinking of someone else kissing my Jessica. I cannot put my finger on just one thing that makes her the one, because I love everything about that girl. Her scent a mixture of jasmine and lavender, not only did it fill my nose I could taste it on her ear, neck, and lips. The only thing that she wanted happen to be me and I didn't understand that when I should have. I wanted to show her what she means to me, and how it will be for the rest of our lives if we stay together.

I traced the back of my hand from her neck down the middle of her chest, but never taking my eyes off of hers. Those deep green colored eyes sucked me in as she looked innocently at me. I could tell she wondered what we were about to do. I wanted to make her want me so bad that she would beg me to make love to her forever. When you love someone it's not just sex, it happens to be so much more than that. Making love is a way to express the trust, loyalty, respect, and dedication to this person that fills every part of you that is missing a piece. Someone once told me that sex happens in mind, not in body. I have found that to not be true for me. It happens in body and mind, not really sure which gives you pleasure for it's a fusion of all senses; love, lust, touch, and a whole lot more.
I slowly lowered the sheet wrapped around her and pulled her to me. Our time to complete the connection happened to be now. I lowered her to the bed moving between her legs wear the warmth of her could rest against me. She smiled as I enticed her with my desire rubbing against her throbbing with need to dive deep within her.
"Jessica, will you marry me?"
She shook her head no, but with the cutest grin on her face. I enticed her more with little kisses against her neck and under her ear asking again, "Jessica, you must tell me you will marry me."
She shook her head *no* yet again.
My ego hurt but determined to make her say she would be mine I brushed kisses against her cheeks while my membrane rubbed against her wet folds. I pleaded again, "Please tell me you will marry me?"

I could see the tears well up in her eyes. She gave me a slight grin as I took the ring from the box and pulled it out. Taking her hand in mine I slid it on her finger, "Jessica, will you honor me by telling me you will marry me?"

She nodded as the tears trickled from her eyes and down the sides of her face. At the moment she said yes I pushed into the depths of her core where the warmth surrounded me. She gasped for a breath of air, but I captured her squeal tasting those sweet lips. Not moving an inch of my body allowing her body to adjust to the intrusion I kissed, sucked, and licked her mouth. The throbbing reminded me of where my penis happens to be at this very moment. As slow as humanly possible I withdrew until just the tip touched her. Her hands trailed down my back until she gripped to pull me into her. Gliding back into her with a little more ease; her body engulfing me pulling me deeper. The tightness of her enticed chills up my spine. Not taking my eyes from hers for one reason only, I wanted to see her face as we made love for the first time.

I wasn't doing as well as I had expected. I had jacked off to build my tolerance for this moment, but nothing compared to the way this filled every dream I had about the first time with her. The warmth of her interior added to the sensation making the release come to fast. I knew she didn't have the same feeling as me because her face hadn't changed at all. I blew it because I wasn't able to give her the pleasure that she had given me.

I rolled over pulling her with me just to hold her to me. As I closed my eyes to cherish this moment with her I promised that I would make it up to her as soon as I regained some energy.

When I opened my eyes she wasn't there. I sat up looking around my room and she wasn't here at all. I looked where we had left our clothes and not only were her clothes missing, but I was still in mine. I still tasted her on my mouth, her scent filled the room, and the sensation still throbbed in my membrane; finding that I had ejaculated in my dreams. It's crazy, God she's mine. Grabbing my phone I made the call yet again.

"Paul?"

"Jess!" My voice betrayed me with a hint of torment.

"Are you okay?"

Subduing the agony I replied with the truth, "No, you?"

"Not really."

We sat in silence listening to each other breath. I know she broke up with me, but for a good reason. I left her lonely and sad most of the time, but I did it for her. She wasn't ready to take that next step and my needs were getting harder and harder to suppress. I wanted to give her time to grow into herself without pressure from me. We're both sad and lonely now, and neither of us wanted to let go. To deal with it we call each other listening to each other breath….

# 1

## *Jessica*

Paul, my ex-boyfriend of three years, happened to be one of the most amazing guys in the world. He had sandy brown hair that always seemed a mess, hazel green eyes that melted me when he looked into my eyes. A great muscular body, an amazing smile; featuring the best dimples that I had ever seen. I am one hundred and ten percent still in love with him, but the last two years of our relationship didn't go so well. In fact it was hard for me. We spent a lot of time apart, because of his business and going to college. Neither of us wanted it to end, but to go through another year of missing him would be too painful. I didn't want to stand in his way, so I let him go. I have regretted it ever since, but I had plans, boy did I have plans!

I tried a date with a guy from school, Greg, another great guy. The problem of me comparing everything he did to Paul happens to be the problem. I still loved Paul when I kissed Greg. My only intention was to see if there could be anything between us. After the kiss, we both looked at each other and laughed. He didn't have it for me and I definitely didn't have it for him. We had the best hug and agreed that we're much better off being friends than anything else. Besides, his kiss didn't make my toes curl like Paul's did. Oh yeah, comparing them again. This needed to stop because it didn't matter anymore. I had to face my fears head on and fight for what I wanted, Paul.

Mom and dad drove me to school. I hadn't told Paul this yet, but I got accepted to the same school he attended. I wanted to surprise him. I needed to figure out his schedule and then I'd find a way to spring it on him.

He turned over all his work to a few guys that he called foremen, and then he also had workers to handle all his accounts. If we have a chance at all it would have to be now when he had the time. All he had to concentrate on is school, and me, of course.

Mom and dad stayed to get me moved into my room. Before they left they wanted to make sure I had everything.

Dad seemed more worried about Paul than me, "Jess, we should stick around and say hi to Paul ourselves."

"Dad, you are not ruining my surprise for him and no, you are not saying hi to him."

Mom had to get her input, "Are you sure he is still interested, Jess. I mean you broke his heart. It is possible that he is dating."

"No, he's not dating. Besides, we still talk a little. If he did date he would have told me. I told him about Greg."

Watching my mom and dad exchange glances worried me a bit. Did they know something that I didn't? My dad and Paul had this weird relationship where they talked like friends. Hopefully they were concerned for our wellbeing. Paul had been through so much in his life already with his last girlfriend dying next to him in a car. Or it might have been the three weeks I wept in my room.

"If you are sure, but I don't want you to be disappointed."

"I won't."

I walked them down to their car; I have my own now. Thank god I wouldn't be stranded at school and if I needed to go home for a weekend I had the means to go. I pushed them in their car and I kept looking over my shoulder worried that Paul may show up to ruin my surprise. The campus happened to be smaller than I believed, and I didn't have a clue what floor he lived on, even though housing consisted of one building.

When I walked back in I went to the director's area in the resident hall and asked what his room number is. They didn't have anyone staying in this hall by that name. Sure that he still went to school here, I wondered why he didn't have a room number.

I went back to my room, where my roommates worked to organize their rooms. We had three bedrooms and two bathrooms, so I walked into the room that I had decided on being my bedroom. When I walked in a girl had already moved in arranging her side of the room the way she wanted. I sat down on my bed and introduced myself. She told me her name, "Karlie Brown. She explained that she's a junior. Getting acquainted I filled her in on my plan. We seemed to get along fairly well.

After about two weeks of getting comfortable I set my mind on finding Paul. Going to admissions proved that he definitely went to school here. Sweet talking the student aid guy gave me what I needed, Paul scheduled, which had to be against school policy. Side tracked with school work; it's harder than I assumed it would be I didn't have much time to work on my surprise. My roommate asked me if I really wanted to find him. Telling her our story she agreed that we belonged together. She even had tears in her eyes at the end of it.

Cross referencing our schedules together, I found that the possibility of running into him would have to be planned out. I tried to fit it in and watched for him, but day after day I kept missing him. I did a glance one day as he drove off and my heart sank. Wanting to hear his voice deeply I called him that night.

"Jess?"

"Hey."

"So, how is school?"

"Frustrating."

"It gets better. Tell me where you are. I'll come visit you."

"No, not yet Paul, but soon."

He chuckled, "You are giving into me."

"A little."

He laughed. We talked about his school too, but he didn't stay on campus, that explained a few things. He lived in an apartment about 2 miles from school. The more he explained the better I felt about surprising him. Matt's his roommate at the apartment. I loved Matt like a brother, so that's perfectly good. He also explained that he tutored other students to make extra money, which makes no sense to me. He already makes enough money from him business. Then he elaborated that he did it mostly to help keep him busy.

That's when I decided on getting a tutor for my classes. One way or the other, I am going to find a way to surprise him and that might be the perfect way. The tutoring schedule listed the time slots open and listed the classes he could tutor in. The only bad thing is that it will be two more weeks before he has an opening. At least with his class schedule and the tutoring schedule, keeping tabs on him would be easy.

I examined his schedule for tutoring every day, but they all seemed to be girls. After about a month of trying to catch up and get a head a little I was going to adventure out. I went to the library and met up with a few girls from my class. Tammy, Sue, Rachel, and Bobby all sat closely together discussing something of interest to them all. I walked up and Sue pulled out a chair for me, "Oh, my god Jess, Rachel's telling us about this tutor she has. I am going to sign up just to have time with him; he sounds gorgeous."

My heart raced as I listened to them talk about him. Everything they described fit my Paul to a T. I sat listening and then observed Rachel getting up, "I am off to put the moves on him today."

I stood up and spoke before I realized what I was doing, "You don't want to do that." I didn't even glance around for him when I spoke out, but I saw him out of the corner of my eye walking into the library. They all stared at me surprised at my outburst, but if I didn't want him to know yet I had to hide. I grabbed my stuff walking away.

"Hey, what is going on with you?" Tammy yelled after me.

I just wanted to get out of there. I was trapped, so I found a home in a corner, but I had to see him. I peeked around the corner. Tammy found me and walked up to me with glaring eyes, "What are you doing? You're acting like a stalker."

I laughed and shook my head.

"Do you get nervous around cute guys?"

I looked up at her and then peeked around the corner, "Do you think he is that cute?"

"YES! Don't you, Jess? Or do you like girls?"

I shook my head as I stared at my Paul.

"Jess, you are seriously becoming one of those weird people sitting here staring like that. You should let me introduce you."

"NO!" I turned back to her, "I'm not good around cute guys. I freeze and get all sweaty, so it wouldn't be good. Can you just come get me when they are done?"

She smiled at me, "We need to get you out of your shell."

I shooed her away from me and peeked back at them. I found a spot on the floor where seeing him through legs of tables happen to be the best it would get. I gaze at him, while keeping an eye on Rachel, too. Time slowly ticked by, but when it had been 50 minutes I saw Matt walk in and up to Paul. Was I ever going to be released from this captivity?

Paul introduced Matt to all the girls sitting at the table with them. My breath escaped me with a huff of frustration; this could be awhile. Picturing myself walking up to them and what reaction each of them would have. Paul would get up moving to me, hug me, and maybe even kiss me. Rachel would rip my head off, and the rest of them would be stunned into silent mouth dropping awe. Not that I wouldn't like it, but I wanted to surprise him in a special way. Not just springing on him like it's no big deal going to school here with him.


# *Paul*


"Matt, this is Rachel and her friend's Tammy, Sue, and Bobby."

Being polite he shook each of their hands. I only hoped that one of them sparked his interest. My ploy to find him a girlfriend didn't look promising, but Matt happened to be one of the greatest friends a person could have. I wanted to pay him back for all the bullshit I put him through over the last few years. The problem with Matt is that his shyness held him back. I had no problem with talking to girls I have no feelings for, my heart belonged to one girl and I am going to marry her someday. Tammy recognized his shyness, "Well, we would introduce you to our friend Jess, but she is a little shy."

Shy would be a good match for Matt, but Jess? My heart dropped to my stomach as my eyes stared at her. My mind drifted instantly to my sweet Jessica, how much I missed her.

Matt worked on his shyness and made an attempt to say, "I am shy too. I would love to meet her."

I am impressed with the change in Matt. He seemed to be trying a little harder, but to find a girl as shy as him would be interesting. Both of them being too shy would be really funny to witness, and to think we would both end up with a Jess. I started to wonder how 'many' Jessica's go by Jess. On a weird hunch I asked Rachel, "What is this Jess's last name?"

I saw Matt turned to me quickly giving me a scolding, but we were both relieved when she said, "Hanson or something like that."

I laughed and shook my head and turned to Matt smiling. He just stood there shaking his head at me. Yes, I'm still hung up on my, Jess. I am still in love with that little girl and I wanted to marry her with all my heart. "So where is this friend?"

She pointed to the back of the library, "So Matt, would you like to meet her now?" I suggested.

He grinned as I pointed in one direction for him to go and I walked the other way. We're going to meet this shy girl that would be perfect for Matt. It's my mission to supply him with the perfect girl. I only embarrassed myself three times saying the name Jess to see if any of the girls I found were her, but they just shook their heads at me.

I went back to the group of girls and set up another time for Rachel to help her with interpersonal communication class, and another later in the week for Math. Sue and Bobby wanted to set a tutor session. They had to go through the proper channels so I gave them my blog to register and sign up for a time. I try to help the students that come first. I took one last eyeing search around the room, and it seemed weird to me. I took one more deep breath and pulled Matt out with me.

We were heading to the truck, "Matt, what is the possibility that my Jess is here?"

"None. She broke up with you, Paul." His words hit a little more harshly than I expected.

"But we still talk and the last time she agreed to see me."

"Paul, no! She broke your heart and it's very unfair for her to do that. You should try dating one or some of these girls you tutor. That Rachel is a hottie."

I huffed, "She isn't Jess."

"No, she is not and that is why you will go on a date with her, and the next one and the next one. You need to get over Jess and even if you don't like any of them at least you're trying."

I got in my truck not happy with Matt, "I still love her."

He laughed, "Yeah, I know, but it wouldn't hurt you to test the waters."

"I don't like water."

"Yes, but what a variety."

I shook my head as we headed home.


# Jessica


I worried if I would ever get out of the library and that bathroom. Why did they come searching for me? I went back to the table and sat down with the girls. Rachel asked, "So, what was that about?"

I laughed and raised my eyebrows, "Just a little shy, especially since they're so cute."

Rachel scrunched her nose, "Good, because the shy one wants to meet you."

I grimaced, "The shy one?"

"Yeah, his name is Matt."

I held back a grin as I remembered this guy wanting to join my family. My mom and dad were easy to talk to about anything, and he took advantage of that. My mind also wandered back to him Val all cuddled up together. Even if he is the best guy in the world he isn't the one for me. Besides I would never date a friend of Paul's even if I didn't still love him. I played along, "Well, maybe someday."

They all laughed at me as I sat back down to continue to work on homework again. From now on I needed to avoid meeting up with people when they were scheduled for a tutor session.

Telling myself to stay away from him when he is tutoring didn't last long. I found myself drawn to follow him, observe him, and study his every move. Pretty soon I would have to have him tutor me, because my obsession was hurting my school work. I needed to figure out the best way to surprise him, because if I didn't, surely I would go crazy. My stomach fluttered as I imagined walking up to him while he was tutoring Rachel. I would love for him to kiss me in front of her; being honest, I would love for him to kiss me in front of them all. It pleased me that his heart belonged to me.

In my private little cove in the library where I spied on him I waited for Paul and Rachel to show up for their appointment. I always arrived a half hour before and left a half hour after they were done. The problem with that, today they didn't show up for the appointment. Realizing it must be canceled I headed for my room pouting. On my way to the dorm I saw him setting up a blanket in the commons, and then Rachel sat down on it. He did the same while Rachel moved closer to him. My hands tightened into fists at my side, my heart raced with anger, and my face flushed with heat. Paul had every right to do this, but I still loved him. This is a little too cozy for tutoring.

Tammy walked up behind me, "Yes, she is making head way with that one."

I turned to her, "This was her idea?"

"Yes, but she said he agreed without persuasion."

I turned to walk around the other end of the building, "Jess, where are you going? You should let me introduce you. His friend seemed really interested in meeting you."

"I'm not feeling well; maybe another day."

I ran up to my room and straight to the window. Tears pricked at my eyes, while my stomach twisted to knots. Seeing Paul with someone else tore her to little pieces. Why had she decided to wait for a special moment? Now someone else had his attention. The pain in my heart felt like a knife had been shoved into it and then twisted back and forth to make sure the pain was excruciating. I should hurry up before he changes his mind about loving me.

What surprised me the most is the kiss. Not even realizing it my hands went to the window, and I must have screamed because it didn't last very long when they both looked up to my window. I fell back onto my bed to whimper, cry, and then sob some more. The only thing that repeated in my mind is *what have I done?*

That night I exhausted myself from crying so long and hard. I broke up with him to avoid the hurt and sadness and all I caused myself was more heart ache. Why did I decide not to tell him that I'm here? Oh, the surprise that I was planning, but had no idea of what it was yet. Great, I screwed this plan up.

My phone rang and I wasn't going to answer it, but I wanted to hear his voice, "Paul?"

"Hey."

"Can't sleep?"

"No."

I huffed.  I was hoping it was from the guilt of kissing Rachel today, "Is there something wrong?"

"Yes... No... Jess?"

"What is it?"

"Nothing."

We fell asleep listening to each other breath.  I knew what was wrong and he felt like I did when I kissed Greg.  It wasn't what I thought it would be.  Just like it wasn't Paul for me, that kiss with Rachel, it wasn't me.

*2*

Discussing my issues with my roommate Karlie hoping she would have suggestions for me, but she didn't have a clear opinion. She listened, nodded, and stared at me not saying much of anything. I guessed she didn't want to discuss my problems.

The weeks seemed to go a lot faster the closer we got to the end of the first quarter. I had to buckle down and really start to study to pass my classes. My classes are hard; the homework impossible, and my wandering mind lands on thinking school isn't for me. To distract myself from school work I follow Paul every day, but that drives me crazy. How many girls does he have to kiss? Kissing Rachel has broken my heart, but now it seems he gives each girl a kiss or two. Spying on him obsessively causes sadness to engulf my daily routine.

By the end of the quarter I stopped talking to my roommate especially after I saw her tutoring session with Paul. She disappointed me, but he wasn't mine anymore. I broke up with him.

Each painful kiss embedded in my phone to remind me that he had done this, and if the subject came up he wouldn't be able to deny it. Scanning through the pictures I noticed a trend. He would meet a new student a couple of times in the Library, then they would meet in a remote spot, kiss, and then all of it would end. No more kisses, no more remote spot, just the Library or they would not sign up with him any longer. Never more than one girl at a time to a remote location, but it would only happen once with each girl.

Either they didn't kiss very well or they didn't do it for him. I hoped and prayed the latter. Knowing him for so long before we were together I had watched him go through girl after girl never really having any kind of lasting relationship. He had good reason though, his last serious girlfriend before me died. They had snuck out late one night to make their first time special. As a teenager he thought, at the time, that sex was very important for their relationship. She changed her mind and they argued as he drove her home. Distracted by the argument they failed to notice the dump truck coming or when it ran into the passenger side of his car. When he told me she gasped his name just before she passed away he had tears in his eyes. With me he never pushed the issue of sex; in fact he loved me enough to wait as long as I needed. The sad part of it is; he promised my dad that I would have to agree to marry him before we took that step. I'm too young to get married, so we're still waiting.

The three years we had been together he had been so good, so why did he go back to girl after girl? He seems unsatisfied with the selection, or he didn't connect with any of them. As I realize that no one would do it for me like Paul, he would also realize the same.

To distract me from obsessively stalking my ex-boyfriend I joined a few clubs. My favorite of the clubs is: "Changing the World." The mission statement said "We will live a full and plentiful life, when we help others in need." This is where I met Iaesha. She's a beautiful girl with mocha colored skin that radiated a glow of perfection. She went on and on about the peace core and how she had plans after she graduated from college to go help somewhere in the world and make a difference. The more meetings I went to the more I distracted myself from Paul. Yes I loved him, and if he needed to move on I loved him enough to let go. Planning and helping others in need gave me a sense of pride. Someday I would make a difference in someone's life. Seriously considering joining a group heading to a remote country on a mission I weighed the pros and cons. My reasoning told me that it would be better than staying here to wallow in sadness.

I should have never said that in front of Iaesha. The next thing I knew she introduced me to a bunch of people who were talking to me like I was going with them on their excursion. Then everything happened so quickly. I had a passport, the flight booked, and my name on the list. So confused of how all this happened in no time at all. When I spied Paul kissing yet another girl my whirlwind brain told me to go through with it. Perhaps not getting phone calls from Paul as often made this more real to me.

As time passed quickly, I had to confirm my plans. Iaesha had everything worked out to a tee. If I joined them I could take my finals early due to the tour leaving late March. So torn on what to do I wanted to consult with the only person that had my best interest at hart. I wanted to be here with Paul, but that showed signs of impossibility. I really sucked at this school thing. Not knowing if it's because I wasn't ready for it or if it's my obsession for Paul watching.

Needing help and advice from someone whom I loved, not wanting to scare my mom and dad, and I didn't want to tell them that I failed at college.

Staring at my phone wondering if I dare call Paul; reasoning it out in my head I came up with needing his advice and his voice in my ear.

That's when I hit the button to call him.

"Jess!"

"Hey." That came out completely opposite of how I wanted it to.

"Are you okay?"

"I think I screwed up Paul."

"Why do you say that?"

"I think I ruined it for us."

"NO, Jess. What do you mean?"

"Have you kissed anyone, Paul?"

Silence filled the phone. At least he didn't lie to me.

His voice more determined, "I have one question for you?"

"Okay."

"Do you love me?"

"Yes."

The tears started to stream down my face. My roommate Karlie walked in and took one look at me then walked out.

"Jess, I have."

His confession didn't take away my misery like I expected it to, "Okay. I love you, bye."

"Jess, wait a minute. You kissed Greg."

Blame, what a mean defense. Covering the mouth piece to hide my sob I tried to get a grip on my emotions, but speaking without gasping or blubbering happened to be impossible at this moment.

"Jess, please. I didn't want to. Matt, just keeps hounding me. He doesn't want me to go back to the way I was when I lost Annie, and it's just..."

Grasping for a breath I bellowed, "What?"

"Shit Jess! I love you, but you didn't want me. Remember you broke up with me. I tried to kiss a few girls, but it's not the same."

Confused with what to say I took a deep breath and tried to get it out without letting him hear how devastating his kissing other girls had made me, "What do we do now?"

I covered it quickly as I lost it again.

"Where are you?"

I sniffled and took another deep breath, "School."

He laughed, "What school? Where?"

"You can't come now, Paul. It's been a really bad day and I just..."

"Okay, when and where?"

"When I am done with classes on Thursday, I had planned to go home. I'll tell mom and dad that I had to stay another day and...."

I took a break to breathe, still holding the tears at bay.

"And what, Jess, anything?"

"Meet me at the cabin."

"Okay, we get done the same day."

"You will be there, right?"

"Yes."

"Paul, I am serious. You have to promise me."

"Jess, I will be there. I promise you."

Scared that he would get side tracked, not show up, or worst of all just blow me off like he had done in the past. If he didn't show up it would be the end to the end, "Paul, I couldn't handle it if you…" I covered the mouth piece again.

"I swear to you; I will be there. I love you."

"Okay, but please don't…"

"Jess, I am going to be there. What time?"

"I will be there by 7 pm."

He laughed, "I will be there by 6:50 pm."

"Are you sure?"

"Oh, Jess. Yes, I am so sure. I have missed you so much."

With the phone on my ear I lie down on my bed listening to his breath heavy and fast against his end. Relaxing a little I took my finger off of the mouth piece and my breath trembled.

"Jess, was your day that bad?"

"Yes."

"Do you want me to stay on the phone?"

"Yes."

"Do you want me to sing to you?"

"No, it will make me sadder."

Listening to him moving around and humming to himself as I laid there listening to him helped me to drifted off slowly.


Pulling off passing my classes I got one A, three B's, and four C's. Not happy with my grades, but I passed. That is what matters the most, next to seeing Paul.

Lying to him about the time; I wanted to have time to set it up the cabin romantically. Chinese food, candles, and Rose petals, this would be a night to remember. My intentions to make love to Paul had other benefits too, like stop kissing other girls. The closer I got to the cabin the happier I became. So close to 6 pm I got busy right away putting the food in the oven to keep it warm. Placing the lit candles all over the cabin and then sprinkling the rose petals everywhere, this would be a night he wouldn't forget. Table is set for two, the dinner candles lit, now for the sexy silk camisole with five minutes to spare. Trying a bunch of different ways to stand to wait for him; I leaned against the counter, then the table. But it didn't seem right so I sat on the table, but it would send the message of desperate need. Next to the couch and lay down, but that said *take me now.* Indeed I wanted to make love to him, but he would have to work to get it. I had to be sure that he loves me more than anything.

After all my poses my nerves twisted my gut. Wondering how much time I had now I glanced at the clock that now read 7:15 pm and in that instant my heart broke. Obviously he's late, which told me that he broke his promise. I tried to convince myself otherwise, but after my persistence of how importance it had been to me. If he didn't show up I wouldn't be able to talk to him ever again. This was my final straw as others would say.

My phone rang so I picked it up.

"Jess, I am running late."

Anger bit out my reply, "I can tell."

"Jess, I will be there shortly."

"Okay." I didn't believe him but I had to know for sure, "Why are you late?"

"One of the kids called me with a problem. Tom hasn't dealt with this so I had to show them how to fix it. Now I am covered in grease and this stupid..." He grunted, "Thing won't budge, but Jess don't leave. I will be there as soon as I can."

"Bye, Paul."

"You're not leaving are you?"

"No, I will wait."

"I love you, Jess."

I don't think he understood that my decision to leave the country happen to be based on this one night. If he didn't show up I would agree to go. I grabbed a blanket and curled up on the couch heart broken. My will to live is gone, my heart is hurting, my mind is telling me awful things; and I have to get away. If I go to a place where people would need and appreciate what I have to offer maybe, I would find purpose in my life again.

Disappointment hit me when I woke finding myself still alone. The candles melted into blobs of wax, resembling my emotions. If it could hurt any more than last night, it did. I blew out the candles one by one and the last one went out when my tear dropped to it. This part of my life is over, the sobs seeped from me as I changed and gathered my stuff. Sitting behind the while unable to see I sat there for a short while trying to compose myself enough to call Iaesha.

My time to commit to a purpose, "I am going with you."

"Really?"

"Yes, I have nothing here that I need to stay for. Thanks Iaesha."

"Yes, I am so excited. We are going to a new world."

"Yeah, that's great. I will talk to you when I get back to school. You can tell me what I need to bring."

"That sounds great." She squealed, "I am so happy you are going."

I wasn't but I didn't tell her that.


I drove to Paul's house with a small bag of stuff. After his mother opened the door her happiness to see me lite her eyes, "Jess, what a lovely surprise. What are you doing here?"

Working myself up to handle this I took a deep breath and gave her a huge smile, "I brought a gift for Paul and wanted to drop it off for him on my way home from school. May I leave it in his room?"

"Sure dear. Help yourself."

After making my way down the stairs I went to work. First of all I pulled down the poster of pictures of us together that hung on his closet door, tucked it between his mattress and box spring. It would be too hard to get that out of the house without his mother noticing. I put up a poster of a girl in a bikini for him instead. Every guy likes the girl in a bikini poster. Next on my list is to erase his computer. There are files and files of photos, even ones that I hadn't seen before. I downloaded them to CD's. After verifying that they actually made it to the CD I deleted them from the hard drive. The wolf pictures were a gift to him so those could stay. Finally, the framed photos. Each one, I lay down after pulling the photo out of the frame. His room was empty of me so I went to the den where I found our prom pictures. One more search of both rooms proved that no more memories of me were left behind. I didn't want him to make a shrine like he did with Annie, his last girlfriend. God I loved him, and I didn't want to hurt him. I convinced myself that everything I did was for the best. Heading back up the stairs with my bag in hand, I hugged his mom. My throat swelled and my body shook. I had to get out of there fast before she figured it out I'm losing it. I kissed her cheek and smiled, but my eyes tiered up betraying me. I hurried out the door rushing to my car. Her voice yelled after me full of concern, "Jess, are you okay."

When I got in my car the tears spilled out, but I waved hoping she wouldn't stop me. Not being Paul's girlfriend meant that I wouldn't see them either. It seemed my life had ended. A loud rap on my window startled me enough to make me jump out of my skin. Slowly turning to face Paul, but relief hit me to see his father. A gasp escaped me as I put my car in reverse and slowly backed away. He spoke loudly as I moved away, "Jess, are you okay?"

I shook my head, and continued to back away waving my goodbyes.

I wasn't going very fast because the tears were obstructing my vision. My next stop, Annie's grave. I wanted to see Freedom and I didn't know how to find her. A whole story in itself it's hard to explain, but the jest of it is Annie came back as a wolf to protect Paul. I think she wanted to make sure Paul could be happy again one day. Too bad it wouldn't be me making him happy.

My phone rang and my heart sank as I picked it up not saying a word. "Jess, where are you?"

Between the tears, and the swollen throat I couldn't talk to him. I would have to say goodbye to the man I love with all of my heart. The pain shot through my heart so I hung up without saying anything at all.

Pulling into the grave yard I found Freedom lying on the grave. I got out running to her and put my face to her fur hugging her. She licked every inch of my face as she trampled around me. Her excitement made me feel loved and wanted, which I needed at this moment. I took off the forever ring that Paul gave me and laid it on Annie's grave. Forever cocked her head hinting at a question. I huffed out, "He doesn't have much time for you either I see."

She shook her head like a dog would. Wondering if it's her answer or shaking out her fur from me patting it down while hugging her. Wanting to spill everything to her couldn't happen. If Paul could understand her like he thought he did, then he would know the whole truth of my plans. Leaving words unsaid; I just didn't want to take any chances of him trying to stop me. I went back to my car after saying my goodbyes to Freedom, telling her I wouldn't be back for more than a year. She followed me and sat in the way of me closing my door, "Girl, I have to leave now."

She didn't move at all. I yelled at her that Paul and I are over and that I had to leave now. I pushed her out of the way and closed my door completely bawling now. My phone rang and I answered it yelling, "WHAT!"

"Jess, where are you?"

"I can't do this anymore, Paul, not now not ever."

"What can't you do?" He sounded angry.

"Paul, you promised."

"I am here, where are you?"

"It's over this time, Paul." I yelled at him.

"Don't say that. I can't live without you."

"You have for the last two and half years, Paul, and I made it easy for you this time."

"This is not easy. I love you and we are going to get married. Remember that, Jess?"

"Not anymore, Paul. I love you, but this..." My voice cracked and sobbing took over. Anger and sadness overwhelming my inner core; I couldn't talk anymore. I sat there trying to wipe my eyes so I could drive, but the tears flowed out faster than I could wipe them.

"Come back, please."

"Paul, I made this as easy as I could. You won't hear from me, and I won't answer your phone calls anymore. I love you." After hanging up I didn't answer as it rang and rang. I started on my way home.

I made it to town and pulled over to cry some more. I must have looked stupid or something because people honked at me. I heard the phone buzz and in my confusion I opened it.

*"Jess, please don't do this."*

I sent a picture of him kissing one of the girls that he tutored. I got another buzz shortly after I sent it.

*"Jess, I told you about it."*

I sent him another one, and another one. I sent him all the pictures I had collected over the last few months before he text me again. His reply wasn't what I expected.

*"Who sent those to you?"*

I laughed to myself and didn't reply. Now maybe he understood why I had to get away from this.

# *Paul:*

Who hated me this bad that they would send her pictures of me kissing someone else? Why would anyone do this? This had to be fixed, but how? Those kisses didn't mean the same thing to me that I felt when I kissed her. She had to see the difference. If I showed her pictures of us together, of us kissing it would be obvious that I loved her. All this would end once I send her photos of us happy together. Running into the house I headed straight to my room as my mom yelled after me, "Paul, did you see Jess?"

I stopped on the stairs and walked back up staring at her, "Jess, was here?"

"Yes, she brought you a gift on her way home from school."

"How long ago did she leave?"

"I don't know. A half hour or so."

Dad walked in full of concern, "Paul, she was crying when she left. She didn't talk to me at all."

Mom turned to him, "When did you see her?"

"When she was leaving I knocked on her window to say hi, but she was crying pretty bad and she pulled out without saying anything to me."

My body trembled with anger. Worried about what she left for me I headed straight to my room down the stairs. Searching my room I didn't notice anything that she had left me. This whole thing's a nightmare; so I called Theo.

"Paul, what's up kid?"

"Um, when Jess shows up there can you call me?"

"Okay, why what is going on?"

"We were supposed to meet last night at the cabin, but I got stuck working and now she is so mad at me that..."

"You were meeting her at the cabin?"

"Yes, but I think..."

"Paul, why would she meet you at the cabin?"

Really frustrated I yelled, "Because, we have been talking and she needed me. It is possible that we were going to get back together, no I KNOW we were going to get back together, but I think..."

He interrupted me again, "So, you haven't seen her?"

"No, and now she won't talk to me. Just, if she shows up there call me."

"Paul, what happened?"

"Nothing! I didn't meet her. When I showed up at the cabin she was gone, but now..." I noticed my picture frames were faced down. I crawled on the bed to look at them as I talked to Theo, "FUCK."

He yelled, "What?"

All my oxygen disappeared from my chest as my world collapsed. All of the photos of us are gone, "Theo, I have to find her, but if she shows up there call me. She was pretty upset... I am worried about her driving."

"What is going on?"

"She took all of my pictures of us. Theo, please call me when she gets there."

"Yeah."

"Bye."

After hanging up I walked to my closet. Taking a deep breath and closing my eyes I opened the door. Calming my nerves with another breath I opened my eyes. Once open my fears came true; all of them gone. I text her quickly, *"What did you do with my pictures?"*

So pissed at her right now that if I did find her I was going to, shit. She couldn't just erase our life together. Heading to my computer to find the pictures again; I could order more. Why would she be so stup... Shit, they were gone too, but in the folder she left a note.

*Paul, I have always loved you and I always will. It will be easier this way. You won't have to be reminded of our time together with our photos. It's time to move on for both of us, and I don't want you to live in the past.*

*Jess*

My gut wrenched in a heaving movement as I rushed to the bathroom.  Dry heaves filled the room as I thought, *what the hell is she doing to me?  Why did she do this?  We're supposed to be together right now.*  Not wanting to waste another minute I called her and let it ring, but this time she didn't answer.

## 3

I grabbed my bags out of the car with my room in my mind. If I could just make it there without interference then I could cry till the hurt subsided. There were two things between me and my wallowing, my dad and mom. Of course they were in the kitchen awaiting my arrival. I figured Paul would call my dad, but with us trying to sneak off alone I thought this time he'd avoid talking to my dad.

Dad came at me right away, "You planned to meet him at the cabin!"

"Now, Theo, give her a chance to get in the door."

Glancing back and forth between the two of them, I had nothing to explain. I swallowed and lost *it* screaming as I dropped my bags and stormed to my room. "Nothing Happened! He Didn't Show! You should be Happy!"

Not hesitating I fell to my bed and continued to cry. There should be nothing left after that long car ride home, but I had plenty left to last longer than I wanted. Mom did come in and check on me once in a while trying to coax me out, but I couldn't get out of bed. The ache in my body and the pain in my heart made it hard to move. Mom tried to comfort me with food but death would be easier than the pain of knowing it's over between Paul and me.

Dad came in one day and sat on the bed and rubbed my back, "Jessica, are you going back to school?"

I rolled to him with a slight smile, "Yes."

"Are you sure you want to do that?"

"I will finish this year. After that I will figure something else out."

"So, it's over this time, you're sure?"

I nodded, "I caught him kissing other girls."

He looked at me squinting his eyes in disbelief, so I continued, "I gave him one last chance to work this out. To explain why or how things should be between us, but he didn't show up."

"You did break up with him."

"Yeah, but I did that because he was too busy and he blew me off for two years dad. You know I love him, but that isn't enough for both of us. My surprise didn't work either. That's when I observed him kissing another girl."

His head tilled while his eyes search my face for truthfulness.

Confirming my actions, "It's not just one girl either, Dad."

With understanding he asked, "Are you sure you want to go back there then?"

"I will be okay now. I have to be."

He took my hand and pulled me up, "Well, if you are going back to school you better get your stuff together."

"Why? I still have time."

"Um… no you don't. You have to be back by Monday."

"What about Christmas?"

"Passed. You didn't even move on Christmas."

"New Years?"

"Yeah, you were crying that day, too."

He pulled me to the kitchen and made me breakfast. Mom went up and down the stairs doing the laundry, but smiled at me every time she passed by me. I had lost a month's worth of time. Mom placed my clean clothes on my bed while I packed my stuff in my bags. I had the rest of the day to watch a couple of movies with them and eat dinner. The depression made room for numbness. This is good considering how lost I am about my future.


## Paul


I tried to call Jess, but every time I did I got her voice mail. It's better this way because I'm lost as to what I'd say. Sorry wouldn't cut it this time. When I called the house phone I talked to Theo. He gave me a hard time after seeing her so miserable because of me. Pleading and begging for a minute on the phone with her he still refused. The impression he gave me led me to understand she's in no shape to talk to me. Hell, I wasn't in any shape to talk to her either. If I could fix this by talking to her neither one of us would be this miserable. But if I didn't talk to her soon I'd lose her forever.

There was no hope for a future with my Jess any longer. From now on we'd go in different directions with no way to change that. At least when we called one another it kept us connected, but not anymore.

Matt came down the stairs asking, "You ready man?"

"For what?"

"School."

"We just got home."

"No, you have been sulking in your room for a month now."

"I missed Christmas and New Year's?"

"Yeah, I had to explain why you bailed on the gig."

Not sure how I lost so many days, my sulking had to stop. I grabbed my unpacked bags heading to the door.

Matt laughed, "You did pack?"

Miserably I glance at him replying, "Never unpacked."

"You need to stay away from serious relationships. They are not good for you."

He's right. I had to get back to school and forget girls all together. I pushed him out and up the steps. Finding my mom in the kitchen I kissed her on the cheek. Turning to me she reassured me, "This is temporary Paul. I know you and you will fix this if you can. I love you."

Wanting to agree with her I nodded, but this time it's going to be different. My focus geared to my music, school, and business.

My dad met us by the truck. He stood there not saying a word making this goodbye weird. He stood near the front of my truck with his elbows leaning on the hood. Making a point that he wanted to talk I moved to lean against the truck next to him. Both of my parents had put up with my depression over the years and I am sure he didn't want to see me like that again. Clearing his throat he spoke, "I liked seeing you happy again." His eyes scanned my face searching for that kid who lost his mind a few years back.

I gave him a slight grin, "Yeah. It was nice."

"I like that little girl. I especially like you with that girl." He hesitated while examining me, but then continued, "You smile when you're with her."

Hitting me where it hurt, a lump swelled in my throat preventing me from replying.

"Sometimes we have to do things we don't want to, but the reward is worth it."

This had to be my dad's way of telling me to find Jess and do whatever she needed me to do? Doesn't he realize that is exactly what I want to do, but I don't even know where she is.


# Jessica


Back at school and thankful for the numbness. Numb is better than complete misery. Now that I stopped stalking Paul I've had a hard time avoiding running into him. It seemed that I dodged him at least once a day, glancing over my shoulder watching for him.

Sometimes I went to eat and sometimes I didn't. Not wanting to be around people much and Iaesha was badgering me that I should be preparing to go. No longer wanting to go, knowing I had no choice now, I hoped that the suffering I'd witness would pull me away from my own.

At the end of February the girls came to my room for a night out. All I wanted to do is get through this last part of school and then to leave this place forever, not go out for a night of fun. There's a huge festival in town called The Ice Gala. At the festival there would be ice sculptures, sled racing, and crowning of the ice king and queen. Later in this old warehouse there would be multiple bands where they could dance to all types of music. It's supposed to be a great place. Sure my roommates are tired of me moping, so they ganged up on me. I am being forced to go. Standing in the shower fully dressed I realized that they weren't giving me a choice. Giving in I washed my hair and body stripping my clothes as I went. Talking myself into it as I stood in front of the mirror I encouraged my nerves, *you deserve a night out. Go for it. It can't hurt you.*

When I got back to my room the girls had clothes laid out for me on the bed, "A mini skirt in this weather?" It is the end of February. They had to be crazy or mad.

Casey, a girl from my English lit class spoke up, "Jess, that is what the leggings are for, they'll keep your legs warm. I brought boots too. You have nice legs and you should show them off."

Rolling my eyes while I dressed didn't help with my attitude, but I did like the top. It was a sliming sweater that hung just down to my butt and had a dangerous V-neck. There wasn't much to show off here, even though I had developed very nice boobs, if you ask me. Next, Tammy worked on my hair, and Bobby did my makeup sitting on the desk in front of me. Afraid of what they had done to me I went to the mirror. More than anything I worried that they made me look slutty, but to my amazement I didn't resemble myself at all. I don't think my own father would have recognized me all mad up like this. It sounded odd to me that I chuckled as they pulled me from the dorm.

At least they didn't make me go to the day events. We were getting there by 7pm, eating, watching the crowning, and then dancing all night.

Finding that I enjoyed most everything filled me with strength that my life would go on after Paul. As much as I needed this I could use a break and find a bathroom. Having a few beers with the girls left me a little tipsy as I wandered from room to room in search of the little girl's room. When I found the bathroom the line stretched down the hall through the doorway and into one of the halls where a band was playing. They're good but the line moved quickly bringing me down the hall and to the restroom.

With everything back in place I put lip-gloss on and went out to search for our group of girls. Again moving from room to room I found smaller rooms where DJ played the music of their choice. Reaching the big rooms where the bands played I found Sue. She had wandered off herself, so we weren't in the clear yet. Taking her to back to the bathroom I waited down the hall. The band that played in the hall next to where I stood had ended their set. The large room filled with a hum of voices until they announced the next band that would play. Sue showed up in time to grab my arm and scream, "We are staying for this one. These are guys from our school and the lead singer is amazing."

She watched the stage while I looked for the rest of our group. The music started and we danced a little, but I never even glanced at the stage. I didn't care who they were because I wasn't going to be here much longer. When something familiar filled my ears my heart began to race, my hands shook, and my knees went weak. I turned to the boy who was singing my song on the stage. The song is the one that Paul wrote for me. I stood there in shock watching him play and sing.

"Jess, dance with me."

I didn't move, I couldn't move. Remembering how romantic it felt sitting in his truck staring into his eyes, as he sang the song to me. The song seemed to pull us together. His eyes searched the room, and then connected with mine. I froze not blinking, not running, or even breathing.

"Oh, my god, Jess. That is him, isn't...?"

Turning carefully to her, "He won't recognize me. Let's go."

He quit singing as we started to walk out. Over the speakers, everyone heard my name flowing from his mouth. I closed my eyes and continued to walk away. That's when he yelled my name again while people booed. We got out the door and I took off at a full run, "Get the others and meet me at the car."

"Jess, wait where are you...?"

Not waiting for her reply. He would never leave me alone to wallow in my sadness if he could prove that I'm here. I ran down halls and through big areas getting lost in people as I made my way through the crowds. He kept yelling, but that pinpointed how close he was behind me. I found a back door guarded by a very large man, and my name wasn't being bellowed out any longer. He put up his arm to hold me from going out the door. Panicking, I pleaded, "There's a crazy guy chasing me and I need to escape from him."

He squinted his eyes at me, "Will you come back another night?" This guy hinted at flirting.

I grinned and batted my eyes, "Maybe, if you're here."

He grinned and opened the door as Paul's voice rang out again. When the door opened I didn't hesitate, and the door slammed behind me as I ran for the car. Thank god, Rachel was waiting there for me.

"Where are the others?"

"I will come back for them. Jess, he must have it bad for you. He yelled so loud everyone in the building knew he wanted you."

"I know, just go. I can't see him... ever."

She drove fast to the dorm and dropped me off at the front door. I ran inside and went to my room sitting in front of the door. I should have never left my room in the first place.

## *Paul*

That's my Jess I am sure of it. That girl had the same face, the same figure, but she had grown up into something more than I remembered. If I get closer, get a good look, I'm sure I can prove that it's her. Questions, so many questions running through my head as I chased her- What was she doing here? How is it that she would be here tonight? "J-e-s-s."

Chasing her through this crowd it's hard to keep her within sight. Getting a glimpse of the top of her head I hopped I followed the right girl. Matt chased me, scolding the entire time, "Paul, it's just your imagination."

I stopped for a second and searched the room for her head to appear again. Matt caught up to me, "Paul, no! You're not right about it being Jess."

More determined than ever, I didn't want him to think it's an illusion. I glared at him, "She is here!"

Getting a glimpse of her over his shoulder I took off again after her, "J-e-s-s."

"Paul, stop. She isn't here. You would have known."

I kept running until we got to a door I thought she ran out of. Gary, the big security guy here, stopped me, "Where do you think you are going?"

"After that girl. She is my girlfriend."

"No, she said a crazy guy was following her. I don't think she would be running from you if you were her boyfriend."

"Gary, that's my Jess."

"No way."

I gave him pleading eyes. He glanced at Matt for confirmation that I hadn't lost my mind again so I turned to Matt too, "Please, you have to believe me."

Matt nodded, "If he says it's her; it has to be."

Gary shook his head, "I can't do it. Girls got to have protection and she's running away from something."

Taking off toward the front doors with a growl, it had to be her. Running through room after room pushing my way through the crowds of people time seemed to stretch out in front of me. If I didn't hurry she would disappear from my life forever. This is my one and only chance to speak with her, to win her back. Shoving through the front doors I ran into the street to search in both directions. Matt came storming out the door behind me and bumped into me, "Do you see her?"

Shaking my head I started to jog in one direction and Matt followed, "Paul, why would she be here?"

It was like a light bulb went off in my brain. I stopped and turned on Matt, "Did you send pictures to Jess? Me kissing other girls?" If he did I would kill him right here and now.

"No! I wouldn't do that. You belong with Jess. Besides the kissing was my idea to stop you from being miserable."

"She sent me pictures of me kissing the girls that I tutored. How else did she get them if you didn't send them?"

He had this puzzled expression on his face.

"Matt, she has been here the whole time."

He shook his head, "That isn't possible."

"Well, then you explain how she got those pictures."

He shook his head more, "Are you sure that's her?"

I ignored his ignorance and headed for my truck. I was going to find her and there's one place to look.

Matt followed, "Paul, where are we going?"

"To the school dorm."

"Why?"

"It's her. I'd know her anywhere and where else would she stay."

We got to the truck but Matt stood in front of me with his hand out. I glared at him, "What are you doing?"

"Trust me. It'll be quicker if I drop you off and then park."

I handed him the keys and got in the passenger side. I tapped my foot the whole way because I would have gone faster than him. Driving me crazy with his old man driving we finally made it to school. Not waiting for him to stop I jumped out and ran up to the dorm. Asking the dorm manager where Jess lived.

She gave me a disapproving glare, "I can't tell you that."

I ran down the hall knocking on doors, "Jess… Jess… I know you are here… Jess… please."

All of a sudden I felt large arm restrain me pulling me back to the sitting area. I struggled but he had me at a disadvantage. My arms locked behind me and he lifted me off the floor.

"Now, Paul, you know better than this. Settle down."

"No, it's Jess. She is here. I saw her tonight. Kevin, please help me."

Matt came running in the door when Kevin tossed me to the couch. He pointed at me scolding, "Settle down or I'll call the police."

I put my head in my hands pleading, "She is here. Please help me?"

Matt sat down by me, "Hey, you have to calm down or you won't see her at all."

I leaned back with my arm over my eyes. Shit, I cannot believe I didn't figure this out a long time ago. I sat silently while Matt talked to Kevin. A group of girls came in acting odd. They looked at me and whispered to each other. Three out of the five girls happen to be girls I had kissed and my body ached with regret. Or were they hiding something. I watched as they walked down the hall and they kept glancing back at me, laughing. They knew something. I glanced over at Matt who was distracting Kevin. Getting up I followed them up the steps they took to the next floor. Following them I peeked to watch what rooms they went in. Matt must have been keeping Kevin distract; no one was coming for me. Listening at each door for Jess, she had to be here in one of these three rooms. I heard crying, sobbing, and then her voice and how frantic she sounded. I knocked, "Jess, baby, please talk to me."

Karlie opened the door, "Paul, what are you doing here?"

"Jess is in there. Please let me talk to her."

She tried to look confused, "Paul, I don't know what you are talking about."

"Don't play dumb with me. I heard her. Let me talk to her now."

Karlie closed the door and I knocked and started to yell to her. "Jess, please. Oh come on Jess. Please, I need to see you. Jess, you should have told me you were here. Jessica Jenson, answer me."

I felt those horrible muscles pull me back slamming me into the wall, "I told you, Paul."

I sat down and cried like I never have in my life. She's on the other side of this door. I was so close to her, but yet she was so out of reach. Kevin and Matt pulled me up and walked me down stairs. I didn't move after that. My mind raced through all those days; how I spent them and what she saw. I remembered one day in the library where I had this feeling like she was there and Matt helped me search the library. Giving up our search with me thinking I just missed her too much.

Matt gave up and went home. I wasn't moving from this dorm until I saw her. Kevin got another call and he was very reluctant about letting me stay, "If I have to come back here tonight you are going to jail."

I nodded, "I will behave."

He ran off and I walked back up the stairs. I sat down leaning against the wall across from her room. I didn't want to disturb anyone so that I would go to jail, but I wasn't leaving either.

# 4

Monday morning Kevin walked down the hall towards me. He pulled me to my feet, "Have you been here since Saturday?"

I nodded, but didn't have anything to say for myself. I didn't want to leave until I talked to Jess. Karlie walked out, and directed us down the stairs to the lounge area. Kevin led me to sit on the couch.

Karlie started, "We need to make an arrangement."

Excitement filled my inner core. Jess wanted to arrange a meeting with me. Kevin sat down by me. Not sure if Kevin intended on restraining me or to prevent any outburst on my side, but the support comforted me. Karlie paced back and forth in front of us as I watched her anticipating how this would go.

She stopped and directed all her attention to Kevin, "He can't stay in our hallway."

As Kevin peeked at me I wondered what this had to do with Jess and my reunion.

Karlie, a furry red, shouted, "Paul, she has to be able to go to class."

This is going to be easy. I leaned back, crossed my arms over my chest, and confirmed, "Fine. As soon as she sees me I'll leave."

"No, Paul, you can't be in charge. Kevin, tell him he is going to hurt her worse if she can't go to class."

Raising his eyebrows with a glance at me, "She is right. You don't want to hurt her, do you?"

That isn't my intention. I shook my head and stared down the hall, "So, what does she want?"

"She wants to go to class without worrying about trying to avoiding you."

She shouldn't be avoiding me at all, "Can you tell her I will go away, but after she sees me?"

Karlie shook her head no. No matter what I said Karlie didn't agree with me and neither did Kevin. Both of us missing classes wouldn't fix anything. Wanting her to stay here at this school happened to be a benefit for me, because I would have time to win her back. Letting them think that they won this argument. I reluctantly agreed with stipulations, "If she will give me her class schedules I will clear out before she needs to go to class and I will stay away until the class is over allowing enough time for her to make it home."

Kevin, more perceptive of my inner thoughts, established, "Paul, she needs to be able to eat, do her laundry, and go to the library. The girl needs her life back."

Not agreeing, I just wanted them to think I agreed, "Fine, I will give her space."

Karlie walked away going up the stairs. I looked at Kevin pulling out the box with the ring. I handed it to him, "She's supposed to marry me someday."

He took the box examining the ring. Handing it back to me, "So, what happened?"

My business had to come first for a couple of reasons, and both of them had to do with her. "I screwed up by not putting her needs first."

As if he understood he grinned, "Okay, we'll figure something out, but you can't make her see you if she doesn't want to."

We both watched Karlie coming back with a paper in her hand. She handed it to me, but waited my scrutiny out.

With careful planning she would have to run into me, but girls are smart. I had to make it sound like I wasn't giving up yet, "I will clear out an hour before she is supposed to go to class and I will be back an hour after she is done with class. I will also give her two hours for dinner, laundry, and whatever else she has to do. That is the best I can do unless she will just talk to me for 5 minutes, it's all I am asking. If she doesn't want anything to do with me after that, then I won't hang out in the hallway anymore."

Karlie glared, "You are incorrigible. What I saw in you baffles me. I guess that will have to do, because she isn't going to see you."

I got up and walked out. I went far enough that I wouldn't interfere with her going to class today, but I had to have one peek at her. I noticed when she came out from the dorm. My heart pounding harder than it ever has, my breathing uncontrollable, my feet moved me closer to her. Wanting to run to her, pull her into my arms, and never let her go again seemed extreme, but I missed her so much. She paused on the walkway scanning the area, making sure the coast was clear. Close enough to see her delicate beauty worn with pain. Her skin had paled, her eyes puffy, and yet her beauty radiated around her engulfing her in a heavenly glow. Okay, so maybe it was the sun coming up behind her, but it wrapped her with its stream of lights. Maybe if I groveled at her feet she would take my ring and be forever mine.

I jumped a mile when a hand gripped my shoulder.

"You promised, Paul." Kevin was standing next to me, holding me still while she escaped me. Holding back until Kevin let go, but then again the experience didn't seem to be enough and my feet moved once his hand let go.

Another grip, this one more firm than the last, stopped me, "No. You said you would let her go to class."

I nodded and observed her walk into the building.


Time to change tactics. I got flowers every day, and placed them by her door while she went for dinner. I tried to contact her every day with a text, but I kept it simple. Like: *"Jess, please talk to me," "I need five minutes," "I miss you," "look great,"* but the one that stopped her was *"will you marry me."*

Another tactic, I left notes on the door in the morning and would wait outside in case she decided to talk to me. I tried to go to class too, but found myself searching for a glimpse of her as I walked from room to room. I quit all tutoring, because all I wanted to do is win her back. The days went by so quickly that today happened to be her birthday.

My gift to her had to be extreme. I called Karlie and made arrangements to deliver flowers to her room. Why she agreed I am unsure, but I'm thankful none the less.

A time from our past, Jess's 18th birthday, came to mind. She had been so angry with me about not spending more time with her. Yeah, I blew that to shit. That day I had bought her flowers to represent our past, present, and future. It took me a while to get them all in her room. Karlie watched as I placed the bouquets of carnations on one have of the room. The biggest bouquet I placed a card with my word- *The carnations a symbol of how many days I have loved you.* On the other side of the room I filled with red and white tulips. This card said- *The tulips a symbol of how many days I will love you.* Ended the gross display of flowers with three bouquets of roses; putting the final card in the middle. Standing there a moment remembering everything about her as he placed the final card that read- *The roses a symbol of everything I love about you.*

With hope that she'd remember their love and forgive him enough to at least have a conversation with him. He'd win her back if she found it in her heart to open back up to him.

Karlie supervised my every move, but her face indicated that this weakened her defenses. I moved to the door, my heart ached with leaving. One last glance at Karlie showed her that I didn't do this to start trouble I only wanted a moment of Jess's time.

She stood there wrapped in her own arms, "You are in love with her?"

Nodding as I stared into her eyes pleading for help. I had to ask, "Is she coming around at all?"

The pains in my heart reflected on Karlie's face as she shook her head no.  Leaving with no argument I went home to shower before heading back to sit by her door.

Matt's edginess made me nervous as he followed me around the apartment waiting for my melt down.  Determined not to let that happen again, I put on my coat to head back when my phone buzzed.  When I pulled it out Matt and I shared in the triumph that the flowers had somehow worked on Jess.  My blood rushed through my body sending a tingling sensation to my extremities.

It was a single text from her, which happened to be better than nothing at all until I read it, *"Thanks for remembering this time."*

My knees hit the floor when the air escaped my lungs.  She's gone and nothing I do will change that.  I had neglected her needs for so long there's nothing left in her heart for me.

Lying in bed not realizing how it came to be that I never made it back to Jess's room.  Confusion filled my head why I didn't have her here in my arms professing my last love.  Matt barged in, "Paul, you either have to stop this or get her to see you.  I can't watch this anymore.  Why do you have to be so over the top about one girl?"

The text from last night filled my brain and that deep gut wrenching twist of lost ripped at my insides.

Matt pulled me to my feet, "I will not allow you to do this to yourself.  Get up and do something Paul."

On my feet I followed him pleading, "Matt, can you talk to her.  Tell her anything she wants to hear.  I need your help!"

He walked out the door.  If he talked to her it might help, but it seemed that I had to do this myself.  If I heard her voice it might help me a little.  I picked up the phone left on Jess's message from last night.  Though I didn't break down like I had last night it still burned deep in my heart.

I decided that her recorded voice would have to be enough for now.  I just needed to hear her voice.

Completely surprised that she picked up, but she didn't say hello either.  What was she doing?  Did she want me to beg?

"Jess?"

"Um, no.  Is this Paul?"

"Yes, who is this?"

"It's Karlie.  I thought you agreed to give her space."

"I am.  I just expected to get the voice service.  Why are you answering her phone?"

The line seemed eerie quiet.  She wanted to tell me something but didn't want to at the same time.

"Paul she doesn't carry her phone anymore. The only time I see her with it is when she calls home, and last night."

All my questions came out in a rolling wave, because Karlie wanted to help me. "Is she okay? Did the flowers help? Is she going to see me now? I can't take this much longer."

"Um. That's the reason I answered the phone. I am a little worried; she has a meeting with the administrator this morning."

"When?"

"She just left."

"Is she having problems with classes?"

"I don't think so. All she does is study. I think she's doing better than the first quarter."

"Is it money?"

"Honestly Paul, she doesn't talk to anyone anymore. She hardly eats. And most of the time I can't even sleep in my room because I can't stand hearing her crying all time."

If she would just see me I'd take all the sadness away from her, "She cries a lot?"

"That would be an understatement. Last night she didn't sleep at all. She sat in the window cell and cried all night holding one tulip."

Trying to process her reaction in my head jumbled together. She's done with me forever, but I wasn't letting her go. I made it harder on her. I had no intention of hurting her further, but my protective side sent me to the Administrator's office. I called Theo on my way there.

"Hey, what's up kid?"

"You could have told me she was here."

"What?"

"She has been here all year and I just find out about it."

"Paul, she was planning a surprise and it didn't go well and then when she came home she was upset. I didn't see the point."

"The point is that I could have been spending time with her this whole year and now I just find out and she won't even talk to me."

"Hey, it was up to her."

"I know, but what is the problem now?"

"What do you mean?"

"She has a meeting with admissions this morning. Do you have any idea what it's about?"

"I have no idea. She hasn't said there were any problems."

"You know if it's money; I can take care of it."

"I don't think so. I paid for everything already and I checked the account last week."

"So, you don't know what is going on with her?"

"No."

"I am on my way there now."

"So, you two are talking?"

"No, but I want to help her."

"Paul, I don't think it's a good idea."

"Well, I guess it's not up to you. I am here and if she needs my help I have to try."

"Boy, I don't want her that upset again."

"I hate to tell you this but she has been this way for a long time now and it's not getting any better. I have to try."

"Fine, but call me. Please."

"Yes, of course. I will call you as soon as I find out what is going on."

"Okay. Love you boy."

I laughed, "Yeah, I love you too, dad."

It's like my second nature went into effect. Becoming the business person; knowing exactly what to do next. If there's a problem I always found a way to take care of it. Jess's problem might just be the thing we need to get us back together. Hell, we were already family. She had to see that we are destined to be together.

Running into the building I came to a halt when I saw her sitting in the office about the sixth cubical down the narrow passage of offices. The glass shielded me from hearing the discussion. I sat down outside the office on a bench with a view of her. Witnessing her aggravation, the gestures with her hands, the shuffling of papers, whatever her problem was it was a big one. After observing her for a half hour I got up and stretched, paced a little then sat back down on the bench. If she needed help she had to know I am here for her. Another forty-five minutes had gone by bringing me to my feet again. This time I went for a drink at the fountain. When I turned she came out the door. Her eyes showed how troubled her emotions were when they met mine. The stare lingered between us, both afraid to make a move. Trying to ease her pain my mouth opened to offer her my help, but nothing came out. I cleared my throat and tired again, but she was already heading to the door.

I ran and stood in front of her, "Is everything okay?"

Her gaze made it back to my eyes and she shook her head no as the tears filled them.

I caused her more pain, "Is there something I can do to help?"

She shook her head pushing forward to get past me, but passed my arms and into my chest with her face hard. Not expecting her to react this way I enveloped her into my arms. I wrapped my hand around her head to hold her to me and wrapped my other arm around her to hold her tight.

Air filled my lungs to the fullest for the first time in months. As I took in the scent of her hair it filled my nose and I buried my face to her head whispering, "Jess, Its okay. I am here now."

Yes, that was the wrong thing to say. She was letting me hold her until I opened my mouth. She pushed me away and started to walk away. I grabbed her and pulled her back to me, "Jess, please tell me what is going on that has you this upset."

Her eyes came back to mine and I wanted to drop to my knees and beg her to forgive me. They were so green but the whites of her eyes red. I let go of her and stared into those eyes. She hit me full force with her body again wrapping her arms around my waist hugging and squeezing me so tight. So confused, so tell me why I'm in love with this crazy over emotional girl. Oh, yeah, I could breathe when she was around.

Lifting her into my embrace I carried her out. She wrapped her legs around my waist and held on to me like her life depended on my hold. When we passed Kevin he gave me nod of approval. I had my Jess back just like that. I whispered to her ear, "Do you want me to take you to your room?"

She shook her head no.

"Do you want me to bring you home?"

She shook her head again.

"Do you want to go home with me?"

She nodded. I was bringing my baby home with me.

"Do you need anything from your room?"

She shook her head no, so I headed straight for my truck. I opened the door and set her down on the driver's seat. She scooted over so I slid in next to her. She laid down right away with her head on my thigh and her face to my stomach. Tracing my fingers through her hair as I drove to my apartment brought me back to our past, our love, and our future together.

Sliding out of the truck I pulled her with me until I could take her into my arms again carrying her into the apartment. The further we got the tighter she held onto me. Finding a chair near the table I sat holding my love. Enjoying every minute of holding her I needed to understand this turn of events. I pressed my lips to her head asking, "Jess, are you going to tell me what is going on with you? I can't help you if I don't know what to do."

She shook her head tucked her face deeper into my neck. As much as I loved that she wanted to be this close I needed to know so I could help her.

"Jess, I need to know. I have to call your dad back."

Everything ended abruptly. She pushed away from me standing up yelling at me, "Why do you have to call him about everything. Shit, Paul."

Confused by this I stood too. If she tried to run I would stop her.

"Where is the bathroom?"

I pointed to a short hallway, directing her to use the one off my room. She stormed into it closing the door behind her. Standing by my bedroom door waiting for her to come out so we could talk, trying to clear my name, "Jess, I called him to see if he knew why you were in the admission's office. I wanted to help, but I promised I would call him back."

She opened the door and stood there glaring at me like I had done the worst thing in the world. Trying for the innocent stare, knowing that I screwed up again, I crossed my arms over my chest. Frustrated with everything to do with her I found myself being short with her, "Jess, what do you want from me? I want to make you happy and everything I do makes you miserable."

She moved to me wrapping her arms around my waist and resting her face to my chest, "This helps the most."

Such a simple gesture, worry filled my chest. With her in my arms I would do anything she asked of me right now.

She peeked over my shoulder, "Is this your room?"

I pulled her to the living room, "Yes, it is but that doesn't fix things, Jess."

She smiled up at me with light in her eyes. Her arms wrapped around my waist again as we headed to the living room. I sat down on the couch, while she climbed into my lap. We sat and held each other silently. I wondered what I should do to help her, but I was so happy to have her in my arms that I didn't push the subject of what's wrong. The silence between us left my mind wandering with a million unanswered questions. The main one being, what made her so miserable that she came to my open arms?

We did well just sitting there, but I lost it when she kissed my neck. I lifted her chin to me and kissed her mouth. Another mistake I had to make because when she kissed me back it released all of my control. I moved to her mouth consuming her. This wasn't a child's game anymore. We were both consenting adult, though I had agreed not to take her virginity until she agreed to marry me, the thought made my loins jump to attention. My hands held her face trembling with wanting to hold her harder to me. In one swift move I lifted her off my lap and lay her down moving next to her so I could feel her whole body against mine. The kisses a playful dance of lust, as I traced mine against hers, nibbled on each lip, and sucked her in for more. Her leg wrapped around my hips allowed a heated sensation against my erection. I felt my body press against hers even though my head was telling me no. If she wants to make love I am not turning her away, that's what I always did in the past to preserve her innocence. With any luck she would get pregnant the first time around and she would have to marry me. Her hand came up to mine and gently loosened my grip on her face. Her lips pressed to mine but then pulled away from me and tucked into my neck. Not sure of what would come next I scooted to my back while she draped her body against mine. Her leg coming up to rest on the over grown hard on in my pants, her mouth found my neck again, but this time she whispered, "I love you, Paul." I pulled her tight to my body pressing my lips to her head. My heart raced, my breath panting from the excitement of her affections. It took a while before I could calm myself taking sweet long breaths against her, holding her. My baby is home, now I had to find a way to keep her here.

When I felt the heat of her breath rhythm against my neck I knew she slept. I wanted to sleep too, but I was afraid this would all end.

Matt walked in and looked at us lying on the couch. He walked over glancing down, "Is that Jess?"

"Who else would it be?"

"I should have known better. I can see the difference in you already."

"What do you mean?"

"You look... happy."

I am happy. I have my Jess in my arms and I could breathe again.

Jess spoke, "Hi Matt."

"Hey, Jess. Glad you're back."

"I was never gone."

"Oh, yes you were to Paul."

She looked up at me and smiled, "I should go back to the dorm."

I shook my head, "You should stay here at least for the night. You can have my room and I will stay on the couch if you want."

She gave me that soft little smile and started to get up from our cuddling session. I held her hand to stop her from moving away from me.

"Paul, like you said this doesn't fix things. I need to go back to the dorm now."

I shook my head not looking at her. My hands trembled as I let go of hers. I put my head in my hands entangling my fingers in my hair to pull it out if she said she didn't love me, "I can't, Jess."

"What do you mean you can't? Are you going to keep me captive?"

I huffed, "If I have to... yes."

She turned to Matt for help, "Matt, will you please take me back to the dorm?"

He laughed falling down in the chair, "I can't either, Jess. I hate to say this but you two belong together."

Her hand brushed under my chin pulling my face upward. I shook my head until my eyes met hers. I would do anything she wants, but let go of her even for a minute.

"Paul, I shouldn't have let this happen. It will hurt more and I can't do that again. Why won't you take me back to the dorm?"

"I'm scared that I won't ever have this chance again."

Determined to keep her here I went to my room grabbing a large T-shirt and a pair of boxers setting them on the bed. When she peeked into the room I pointed, "There, you can sleep in that. You can have my room and my bed. I will take you back early enough to get to class."

She tilted her head, "This is going to hurt worse, Paul."

"I don't care. I am not letting you go."

Not wanting to hear her say no I stormed to the living room, sat down on the couch, and folding my arms on my chest.

## Jessica

Picking up the T-shirt taking in the smell of him that lingered on it. My heart grew with comfort with his scent. It wasn't sweaty; more of a manly scent of working outside, but a hint of musk cologne. After changing into the T-shirt, I pulled back the covers and crawled across his big bed into its warmth. My reward for caving to Paul's open arms. Not a hard mattress that creaked of plastic every time you move. Tracing my hands over his sheets and up to the pillows, grabbing one I sat back up pulled it to my face and inhaled his scent again.

The guilt that overwhelmed me about Paul already hurting, how would he be able to handle me leaving for a year? I wanted to tell him, but I couldn't. He would never let me go, but I had to now that I agreed. Plus, maybe seeing others hurt and suffering would make mine seem foolish. At least that's what I hoped. This is my opportunity to find anything else that I had to get rid of. Not finding anything in his drawers or in the closet to remind him of me satisfied my curiosity until I turned on his lap top finding a huge picture of us together. Stopping at his house to get rid of our relationship didn't get rid of everything. This all had to go before I left. It would be easier if he didn't have to be reminded daily of me. I went back to the bed and heard a knock on the door. Covering up a little I answered, "Come in."

This amazing good looking man walked in with eyes on me. That crooked smile on his face as if he's up to something. His eyes so worn; I supposed that's my fault for not seeing him. He did sleep in the hallway for almost two weeks. He walked to his dresser and took out shorts and a muscle shirt, "Just grabbing clothes, Jess, and then I will leave you alone."

I sat there watching him search slowly to get things out. I knew he hoped I would ask him to stay, but if I did the pain would be so much worse when I left. It isn't about what I wanted or needed, it's about protecting him the same way I protected myself. I didn't want him to hurt deep down in his gut, like the world would be better without him, the way I do every day. The knowledge of me leaving and not seeing him killed me a little more each day. I thought about the meeting with the administrator. He advised me that I'd pass my classes based on my homework and I wouldn't have to take any finals due to volunteering to help a third world country. The whole time he had talked to me I focused on not seeing Paul, not hurting him, and no more pain and suffering for me.

While not paying attention to Paul, lost in my own world, I heard my name on his mouth, "Jess,"

Catching me off guard I jumped, "Yes,"

His eyes were so caring, as they stared at me, "Are you okay, really okay?"

Trying to hold it all in I nodded, but my eyes stung threating to tear up. All I thought about now days happen to be the man who stood in front of me now. How I wanted to give into letting him have my heart, but with me leaving the pain I would cause him. I had to protect him from hurting again.

He came to sit on the bed and traced his hand along my cheek, "Please let me help you. Tell me and I can help fix whatever it is that has upset you."

I reached up and touched his chest and gazed into his eye, "My sadness is from missing you, Paul." I didn't lie.

The slight grin washed from his face but his eye didn't leave mine, "Why didn't you tell me you're here? We could have had the whole year together."

"I planned on surprising you, but you didn't live on campus so I tried to spy on you to find out where you lived. Then school seemed to get harder and harder until I got side tracked, and then I witness you kissing someone else. I thought you moved on, and then when you didn't show up at the cabin I came to terms with that and I couldn't put myself through it anymore."

"I am not over you and I will never be over you. I love you and want to marry you." He got up and grabbed the white box and came to sit on the bed. "Jess, this will keep us together forever. All you have to do is say yes."

"I can't, Paul, not yet. I still have something I have to do."

"Can we do it together?"

"Not this, Paul. When you didn't meet me I agree to..." Choking on the words the crying took over and I couldn't finish what I needed to say. I fell back covering my face bawling. There's no way to change my future for the next year. I'm leaving him and my heart pounded to near explosion from the sadness that engulfed me.

He crawled over me, "Jess, what did you agree to do?"

I rolled away from him curling up to a pillow hugging it. He lay down beside me wrapping his arm around me.

# 5

I woke to Paul opening the curtains with the biggest grin on his face. He's so cute with his messy hair in the morning. He pulled back the covers and grabbed me by my ankles pulling me to the edge of the bed, "It's going to be a great day. Come on sleepy head." When he let go I rolled over and crawled back up to the pillows, "I'm not going. I like sleeping in a real bed."

Laughing and pulling my ankles till they dangled off the bed he dropped them, and grabbed my wrists to pull me to sit up on the edge of the bed. The next thing I knew I was flung over his shoulder. I pretended to be a limp rag. He moved around the room and walked out. I reached up grabbing the shirt to cover my butt. Paul held Matt's door closed as we went by it.

"You can put me down now."

He laughed walking into the bathroom.

He set me down in the tub and I glared at him. "I need to go to the dorm."

He opened the medicine cabinet and set my shampoo and conditioner on the toilet. He smiled and pulled out spritz spray and then he bent down and pulled out a blow dryer. I shook my head surprised that he has all my supplies here at his apartment.

He walked over to me smiling, "You need to wake up first."

He turned on the cold water making me screamed, "You jerk that is freezing." I reached for the hot water.

He backed out of the bathroom, "Remember, Matt is here and you..." He looked down at me, "are wearing a white T-shirt."

After he backed out closing the door I looked down to see what he meant. Yep, completely see threw. War of the Roses came to mind, how I would get back at him. I took the shirt off and then the underwear wondering what he was planning on me wearing to the dorm to get my clothes.

## Paul

I want to keep her here so she'd see what it would be like to live with me. My hope for her to like it here replayed in my head over and over as I went to make breakfast. She had to be happy here to stay with me for the rest of our lives. Matt stumbled out, "You slept with her?"

I glared at him, "Yeah, we slept!"

"You're happy?"

"Yes, I am. Do you want breakfast?"

"You're cooking, yeah. What was with the screaming?"

"I put her in the shower and turned on the cold water."

He laughed, "She's the type of girl that will get revenge."

"Jess, no. She wouldn't do that."

He laughed out loud. I finished and made three plates. I ran to the bathroom, "You take longer than I remember."

She opened the door and I backed away. With only a towel on, she walked across the living room to the table. Matt's mouth hung open. I walked over to him and hit him in the back of the head to remind him he was staring. He choked, "I'll finish this in the living room."

He picked up his plate and moved to the couch. Jess looked down at the table so I asked, "Are you hungry?"

She smiled and walked towards me, "Are you?"

Confused, and a little irritated, "Jess, Matt is here. You should get dressed?"

She laughed, "Yeah, and what am I supposed to wear for underwear?"

I shook my head and laughed with the thought *Commando.*

She walked up to stand directly in front of me, "I bet you didn't think about that when you put me in the shower."

I smiled at her with the biggest grin shaking my head no.

"Besides, someone else may need a cold shower." She opened the towel in front of me making my heart pound so hard I heard it in my ears. With every intention of staying in control I concentrated on her eyes, but when she moved my attention move south. What a perfect body. Her breasts were the right size to fill my hands or my mouth, either fine by me. My eyes still wandered further south when she swished her hips. Her waist thin, milky, and smooth; I could play for a while with that belly button. A throbbing in my groin my eyes ventured further over her body almost to the sweet spot when she dropped the towel. I grabbed it quickly wrapping it back around her pulling her against my body.

It might sound like a growl when I yelled, "Matt!"

"Yep, I'll eat this in my room. I told you, Paul."

"Woman! What are you trying to do to me?"

Dancing with sparkle her eyes met mine. Her mouth parted just slightly when the corners of her mouth twitched to a smile. When her hand stroked against me I closed my eyes. If she wasn't careful I would do it right here on the table, take her like breakfast.

Her giggle; a painful delight, "Told you someone else needs a cold shower."

She took the towel from my hands and wrapped it around her and sat down across the table from me. She crossed her legs and sat there smug and took a bite of a piece of bacon. I walked over to her and leaned down to her ear, "You are cruel."

She laughed, "You're the one that wanted to see me in a wet t-shirt, Paul."

She's right I need a cold shower after that display. That's pure evil on her part. This is going to be fun. I have five weeks to win her over before school's done and it's going to be the best five weeks of our lives.

After a shower and dressing I worked on a wardrobe for her to leave the apartment in. As I set out a few things she strolled into the room.

## *Jessica*

Oh my god he's gorgeous. Standing here in front of me in nothing but a pair of jeans hanging low on his hips tempted me to touch. A fine cut man he has grown into with ab muscles that rippled, oblique's that V, arms that bulged without flexing. No wonder they couldn't keep their hands off of him, he took my breath away.

"Jess, I hope this is okay. You'll have to go commando until you get to your dorm." The thought made me grin from ear to ear. Taking advantage of the situation he continued, "Maybe you should bring some of your things here?"

I grinned but I shook my head. This is all going to be over in two weeks when I had to leave for South America. How could I let this go on knowing that it will be so painful for both of us? Realizing that I'd hurt the man that I loved. I needed to behave and push him away gradually. Maybe I should be a pain in his ass so he wouldn't like me anymore. There are so many things that I loved about Paul, like the way he looks at me, the way he touches me, the way he holds me, and most of all the way he loves me no matter what I do.

He moved around me intending on leaving the room, so I turned to watch as he pulled a shirt over his head. He glanced back at me grinning, "You have to hurry or you are going to end up going to class without anything on under that."

With that grin of his, how am I going to push him away?

We walked up to my dorm room hand in hand. God I missed this so much. He waited in the living area while I went to my room to change. When I came back out he was helping Karlie with something in her school work, but stopped immediately when I came out. His face went white with fear that I was going to be angry and Karlie turned to me, "Jess, he is such a good tutor; you should let him tutor us still."

Laughing with a sigh when I replied, "I didn't make him quit. You have to ask him." Our eyes met with challenge.

I wanted to know if he'd choose me, or if he had to do more with his life. His challenge happened to be me or work.

He gave me the crooked little smile but spoke to Karlie, "No, I can't. I have neglected Jess way too much. I need to have more time to spend with her."

It put a smile on my face to hear him say that, because we only had about two weeks and then it would be over again.

He held out his hand for me to take, "Are you ready?"

I nodded and took his hand following him out of the room. We walked to class together, "Jess, I will be waiting right here for you when you are done."

"Don't you have class or something?"

He raised his eyebrows, "Yeah, something."

I rolled my eyes and shook my head as I let go of his hand to walk into class. He pulled me back, "Aren't you going to kiss me?"

I raised my eyebrows teasingly, "You think I want to kiss you in public, Paul? People might get the wrong idea."

"That's the idea. I am in love with you."

I smiled embarrassed as a few people walked pass me into the room. His hands came to my face and he kissed me passionately. He took my breath away and he gasped as I pulled away. Oh, my goodness, I am so in love with him all over again. I walked in backwards staring at him, "You'll wait for me?"

He nodded with the most pitiful face. Being apart for this hour and a half is going to be torture.

After the school day I went to my dorm. He was still in class but I put a bag together. Karlie walked in, "I thought you were lying to me about Paul, and you were fantasying about the guy."

I laughed, "We have been together for four years, except this year, but our hearts still belong to each other."

"So why did you break it off with him anyway. I'd never let that one go."

"He was too busy for me, and it made me sad all the time, but now I wish I didn't have to leave."

"Iaesha?"

I nodded.

"Does he know?"

I shook my head. "I gave her my answer when he promised me he'd meet me at the cabin and then he didn't show up so I said yes."

"He looks at you like he is in love with you."

"Yeah, I hope so, but he gets busy and I need more attention than what he gave me. It's always a competition with his business, his first love."

"Are you going to tell him?"

"Not now. He won't let me go and now I have to go."

"He is going to be heartbroken."

"Me too. I love him with my whole heart."

"Yeah, I noticed."

"Please don't tell him; let me when the time is right."

She nodded as he came storming in, "Jess!"

I held my bag up, "Just getting a few things in case I end up in the shower again."

Karlie laughed, "Getting right to it I see."

"No!" Paul said with disgust, "She needed to wake up, that is all."

He took my bag and my hand. My heart thud a little faster. I'm in heaven. On our way back to his apartment we stopped to picked up dinner for three, not leaving Matt out. Paul said if he didn't make Matt food the guy would never eat. He doesn't cook.

We ate dinner the three of us and I detected a funny grin on Matt's face all through dinner. I nudged him with my foot to get him to stop but he kept smiling and would giggle to himself a little now and then. Paul and I made plans for the whole week and our time together. I knew that all my free time would be here with him. Trying to push him away slowly wouldn't happen; I needed him so badly right now. We moved to the living room where we did our school work, but I finished first. Now with my school work done I stood up and put it away. Reaching over the back of the couch I tickled Paul's ear. He shooed me away, but I persisted on attention and whispered in his ear, "I need time." He grabbed me and pulled me over the couch to his lap. When his eyes met mine they were full of desire for me. He needed play time too. Gesturing to Matt still studying, Paul let me get up. Matt got the hint without us asking. He stood up sighing, "I guess I am going to finish in my room."

Crawling on the floor towards him I pulled on his leg, "Matt, please don't leave us alone."

He shook his leg, "Jess, stop it."

I stroked his leg leaning against him, "You shouldn't leave us alone."

Paul grabbed my legs pulling me back to him, "Yes, he should." Crawling over me he pinned me down as he hovered over me.

I reached again, "Matt, help me."

"No, I like when you two are together. Sorry, Jess, you will have to fend for yourself."

He walked into his room and closed the door.

Grinning from ear to ear, Paul is mine for the rest of the night.

His body pressed to mine the arousal evident. Possible this is the night we show each other how much love is there.

His fingers touched my cheek, "Do you like to torture me?"

A little nervous with the inclination of making love to Paul I shook my head no and pushed for him to get off me. He sat back watching me get up, "So am I on the couch tonight?"

Shrugging while walking away to the bed room I closed the door behind me. I needed a couple of minutes to compose myself. After changing into sleeping shorts, yes they were really short, and a camisole that sat just above my belly button I walked back out making my way around the couch to Paul. He sat on the floor with his legs stretched out in front of him crossed at the ankle just viewing the TV. Stepping over him to demand his attention he didn't hesitate letting his eyes trail up my body. His hands not able to stay off me traced my calves. I sat down on his lap facing him. Admiring his features I ran my fingers against his forehead, and then traced them down his cheek. He gazed deep into my eyes and gave me that great smile. My fingers found a dimple and I traced my fingers deep in it. A touch of embarrassment touched his face as his gaze dropped from mine, "Jess, are you going to marry me?"

I whispered, "Someday Paul."

His eyes came back to mine full of worry, "You still love me, right?"

I wanted to show him how much, "I have always loved you, Paul." More determined to make him understand I held his face to mine, "And I will always love you. Just sometimes we let other things get in the way."

He agreed, "Then you need a cold shower little girl."

Heaving my chest in front of him hoping he would notice how much I have changed, "Are you sure I am a little girl, Paul?"

His hand came to my chest and his finger slipped under the edge of the camisole tracing it down to the cleavage. He was shaking his head as his eyes followed his finger, "Your right; you're not a little girl anymore."

Taking his hand in mine entangling our fingers together. I laid my head to his shoulder with my nose along his neck so I'd smell him. He wrapped his arms around me, "Jess, what is it that you have to do?"

Nudging his neck before I pushed to get up, "I don't want to talk about it Paul. Can we do that later?"

He watched me as I put out my hand for his. He followed me to the bed room, but stopped at the door waiting for me to tell him what we were doing.

I pleaded as I noted the gaze on his face, "Can you sleep with me?"

He smiled and crawled onto the bed next to me. I curled into him tracing my hand up and down his chest watching him breath. He stroked my arm and kissed my head. He'd have night mares tonight. He always did when he worried.

# 6

The nightmare did come in a wave of whimpers and body twitching, but I soothed them by whispering in his ear, "I am here Paul."

Back before he and I ever had a relationship his girlfriend had died when a garbage truck ran into them. She had gasped his name as her last word. The guilt he carried haunted him for so long. My dad had given him hope by hiring him to help with our cabin, and then referred him to others. That is how he started his business. He would sometimes stay at the cabin with us. At first I would hear him in the other room, but after we got to know each other he would come to my room and fall asleep sitting up next to the bed with his fingers barely touching me.

After he figured out that I would wake when he came in he started sleeping on the bed with me. I would run my fingers through his hair to sooth him; sometimes I would just wrap my arms around him to hold him. It wasn't until we started dating that dad put a stop to that, but if he had a bad dream he would still show up and I would still do what I could to comfort him. He always told me he slept better when he could hear me breathing. Nothing ever happened when he would come into my room, except the need to sleep next to him.

I wanted to wake Paul the same way he woke me the other day. Sliding from the bed I snuck out and started breakfast. When I had a couple of pancakes done I knocked on Matt's door, "Time to eat."

"What?"

"Matt, it's time to eat."

As I heard him get up I went back to Paul's room opening the curtains. Not having to say get up to him, because he already pulled a pillow over his face. Yanking down on the covers my eyes took in every inch of his amazing body. Hearing me giggle to myself he peeked from the edge of the pillow, "What are you giggling about?"

I bit my lip, "You're not a little boy."

He rolled over covering his head more. I crawled over him and rubbed my hands up his back, "Did you need to stay in bed today?" I leaned down and kissed his back.

When he rolled to his back he took the pillow from his head and covered himself.

I giggled more witnessing his morning hard-on.

"You don't want to kiss me like that unless you're asking for it."

A rise my eyebrows with the biggest grin on my face I teased, "I am asking for it, but the stove is hot and ready."

Quickly I scooted to the end of the bed pulling him by the ankles; he didn't budge an inch. He laughed and threw the pillow at me, "Out, unless you plan on helping me with this."

I ran out of the room. Matt filled his plate as I came back to the kitchen moving to the stove I flipped the pancakes. He shoved a huge bite in his mouth, "Jess, are you moving in with us?"

"NO!"

"I don't mind. So far I've had breakfast every day that you've been here."

Finding his logic humorous I sighed, "But you had to study in your room."

With all joking aside he asked, "Are you happy here?" Not waiting for my response he continued, "Paul is happier with you here."

Not answer him the pain shot through my heart knowing I would be leaving soon and it's going to hurt him again. My stomach turned. I avoided answering him by finishing the pancakes on the stove, washing a few things in the sink, setting a plate in front of Paul. Then I escaped to the bathroom for a shower.


# Paul


"Jess, aren't you eating?"

She yelled *no* from the other room. Matt avoided my questioning glance so I asked, "Did something happen, that I don't know about, that would piss her off?"

With eyes filled with apology Matt caved, "I asked her if she was moving in here. We were joking about her making breakfast. I like her here and I told her you are happy too." He leaned over the table towards me and lowered his voice, "It's like I pissed her off or something. Her mood changed in an instant and she got all quiet. Maybe I hurt her, but I didn't mean to upset her."

That's how it went with her. One minute playful and fun and the next she'd put up a brick wall. We had to be more careful around her. Leaning forward I filled him in, "She says she has to do something and she won't tell me what it is she's doing, but my intuition tells me she is leaving."

"Well, we all are. School is almost done."

"No, it's more like she is leaving for the summer, but she won't talk to me about it and she gets sad and defensive whenever I ask about her plans."

"I'm sorry, Paul. I just wanted her to know that I like her being here too."

He liked her here for one reason, "Yeah, you like being fed."

"Dam right."

"Dam right, what?"

When I glanced back up at her she tapped her foot and put her hands on her hips. She's adorable when she is angry. We didn't help the situation because we both cracked up laughing. Matt stood up and put his plate in the sink and jogged toward her, "Dam right I like when you're here with us. You both cook and feed me. What is there not to like about that." He passed her smiling, "My turn in the shower."

She watched him go in his room smiling. Her gaze came back to me questioning, "That's it?"

My voice hinted at laughter with my reply, "Yeah. He likes a full stomach."

She walked over to me and knelt on the chair across from me. She was smiling so she didn't stay mad for long. I grinned at her waiting for her to say something as I ate. I took a huge bite, but couldn't wipe the grin from my face as she stared at me.

"Do you want milk?"

She was going to wait on me, so of course I agreed that I wanted a glass of milk. I eyed her getting up and getting me a full glass of milk. When she walked over to me and sat on the table, she pushed my plate out of the way. This new forward girl sitting on the table made my groin pulse, "I guess I am done?"

She grinned handing me the glass of milk and scooted in front of me. I drank the glass of milk keeping my eyes on her, but traced my hand up her thigh.

Fingers traced through my hair. My eyes locked on hers to see what she's going to do. With her you had to expect the unexpected. Her face grew to a mischievous grin and then a full smile. She huffed with a little laugh as her eyes sparkled, and then she asked, "Do you want to skip and spend the day with me?"

Who wouldn't want to do *that*, "Yes."

She was giddy, but it hit me like a brick wall and I cringed as I continued, "Shit, I can't, not today. Can we do it tomorrow and make it a long weekend?"

Her smiled disappeared a lot faster than it had grown, "I can't. Not tomorrow."

She started to move away from me. I gripped her arm, "Just a minute, Jess, we can come up with something. Give me a minute to think about this."

She did stop moving away from me, but if I didn't come up with a great idea she would think something else came before her. It wasn't like that for me not any more. I just had things that needed to be done on someone else's time line. It's not a question of what I wanted to do. It's about what I had to do or I'd have done everything to fit around her, "Jess, stay here a minute. I am going to grab my schedule; I just need to look at one thing."

When her lip came out, my knees went week. Pressing her against the table, "Stay here I just need one minute."

Blinking away the tears that already started to well in her eyes she nodded. Darting to the bed room I collided with the chair stubbing my toe, yelled and danced off into my bedroom. In the other room I could hear her giggle. With a limp I hobbled back to the kitchen where she sat waiting with her hand over her mouth and eyes wide with surprise.

Her words came out muffled as she asked, "Are you alright?"

Sitting down in front of her I set my schedule in her lap, but glanced up at those wide questioning eyes. "Yeah, I'm alright." Grasping her legs I pulled her feet to rest on my thighs. Concentrating on the schedule I ran my finger down reading each entry. Her toes gripped at my legs distracting me. I peeked up at her grinning. She has no idea how bad I wanted to toss my schedule to the floor, lean her back on this table and finish my breakfast; Jessica with a cherry on top. Shaking off the temptation my eyes scanned the schedule again finding what I was looking for, one test in my 10 am class. Weighing my options, stay here with Jess or take a test. Regretting my discussion before I even mentioned it I took a deep calming breath. Not wanting to see the disappointment in her face, I confirmed, "I just have to go to my 10 am class." As tone as she is her leg muscles flared a gut sensation told me she didn't like my answer. Gripping her thighs once more I pulled myself between her legs. The scent of the sweetness that lingered between them gave me a full hard-on. If I didn't move soon I'd be toast. My eyes began to water from the pain of need. Taking a chance I peeked up at her, "Please tell me that's okay."

The smile crept back along with the pout. I couldn't help myself but chuckle a little she's so adorable.

My breath caught when she asked, "Should I go to my morning classes then?"

I shrugged my shoulders, "I guess whatever you want to do. We could meet for lunch and then what ever you want to do."

She took my schedule away setting it down on the table. She scooted forward and ran her hand through my hair pulling my head back, "I have issues with asking you to promise me something."

I didn't know how to take that and I didn't know what to say. She moved her feet off of me and slid down to my lap. She wrapped her arms around my neck and tucked her face into my neck whispering, "If I am going to class you need to get ready."

I picked her up as I stood and headed to the bathroom. She moved her face so I could see her smile. Resting my forehead to hers, "If I am going to get ready either you have to let me go, or you are coming into the shower with me."

She let go but I didn't. I'd be happy to have her company in the shower. Reaching for those sweet tasting lips I moaned while I nibbled them. Her hesitation as I let her go she inquired, "Why do you do that?"

With raised eyebrows, "Because you're sweet."

She glared at me and let go running into my room. I watched her grab something from her bag and put something on her lips on her way back to me, "Like this." She kissed me with her whole mouth as I licked her lips, but I shook my head. She released me confused, "That's not it?"

I shook my head and tipped her back sucking her neck and kissed her up to ear, "That's it. You entice me, your sweetness."

She giggled and pushed me away, "Go take a shower, and hurry. If I am going be on time for class we have to hurry."

I laughed and kissed her and then went into the bathroom. My mind drifted to her over and over again in the shower; the little pout, the taste of her lips, and the pulse in her neck. I had to shutter to shake off what I wanted to do to her. It didn't work because I thought about her legs and running my hands along them, tasting her stomach as I kissed her. Okay, she's definitely a woman now, so why are we waiting? Oh, that's right, I want her to marry me and I promised not to do that until she agreed to it.

We were heading to class and I pulled her to a stop outside the room, "I will see you in a few hours. Will you meet me at my truck?"

"No."

"No?"

"You have to pick me up like a date."

"From where?"

"My dorm room, and don't be late or I might not be there."

"You wouldn't!"

"Don't test me."

She walked away from me and leaning forward I almost fell over my own feet. She knew how to drive me crazy.

When I finished my class, I ran the whole way to the dorm and up the stairs to her door. I knocked and one of her roommates answered, "Jess, please." I huffed and gasped for air. She came to the door with another bag full of stuff, "Why are you panting like a dog?"

"I didn't want to be late."

She laughed, grabbed my shirt, and started walking pulling me behind her. We ran into Kevin, the security guy, on our way out. "Hey, how's it going with you two?"

Jess turned to me and gave me that disapproving look.

"Jess, he kept me from camping out 24/7 at your door."

She turned back to him, "Thank you. He is a little obsessive."

Kevin laughed as she pulled me out the door. I wrapped my arms around her waist and picked her up twirling her around, "So what are we doing?"

"You said we're going to have lunch."

"Okay, we'll have lunch. What do you want?"

She grinned at me crawling in the truck. She was going to drive me insane with her facial expressions. I had to shake it off once again and move on with our day.

We stopped after lunch and picked up movies and snacks. Next we headed to my apartment for a day of cuddling, movies, and whatever else we come up with. I hoped for the last. She's so playful watching the movies and eating our snacks. She tried to throw M&M's in my mouth. I fed her cotton candy on my fingers. We cuddled and had chips with dip together. She moved around a lot so I just observed her as she did different things. When she lay down on the opposite side of the couch I took her feet in my hands and started to message them. Touching any part of her pleased me. She leaned back closing her eyes and we heard Matt coming in the door. He took one glance at the room with disgust, "You two are cleaning the apartment."

Choking out a laugh, because I did all the cleaning anyway, I rolled my eyes. Not giving us any more thought he went to his room mumbling.

Jess asked, "Do you think he is irritated?"

"Yeah, probably."

Leaning over the back of the couch to see that sexy little body make its way to Matt's room, I ached with need. After she knocked and he opened the door she dragged him back to the living room, "You my friend, need relax time."

Enjoying the view of her I waited to experience her next move. Pushing him to sit on the couch she held up an M&M.

Matt quickly turned to me with a questioning stare. I shrugged as one came at his face ricocheting off his face. In her scolding voice to demanded, "Matt, you're supposed to catch it in your mouth."

He was shaking his head as she threw another one at him. I stood up and grabbed a handful. Tossing one at him made him yelled at us to stop.

"Jess, show him how to do it." When I tossed one up she caught it in her mouth with ease. His eagerness to be part of our little playtime he caught one in his mouth. We ended up feeding him everything trying to get him to catch it with his mouth. After pelting Matt over and over with M&M's we settled down for a few games of Rummy. As the night crept upon us Matt migrated back to his room leaving us alone again.

Being alone with Jess happened to be my treat for putting her first on my list. We sat down to enjoy another movie as I put my head in her lap to be as close to her as possible. Not that the movie's bad, but I am with Jess and all I wanted to do is take in every second I can. Delicate fingers ran through my hair relaxing me to a light nap. When the touch didn't fill my needs any longer I curled into her more to take in her scent of sweet vanilla, with a touch of spice. The sensation didn't resemble anything that I could remember, but my mouth watered anyway. Tugging her tank top up just a tad so that when my mouth made contact with her skin I could savor what lingered for hours. Her fingers tightening in my hair which made me aware of her tense body. Nuzzling to her core I traced her stomach with my face making her body ridged. Could she be nervous to let me touch her this way? She pushed me trying to get out from under me. Pressing her back down I crawled over her pinning her to the couch. Seducing her into telling me what she had to do might just work. She wanted me now, and wanted me badly, I could sense the need in her body.

Staring into those beautiful green eyes I traced my fingers along her cheek, "Are you going to tell me what you have to do?"

While pushing to get away from me she scolded, "Do you want to make me sad?"

Not wanting this to end I held her tighter preventing her from moving, "I just want to experience everything about you, baby."

"Yeah, and baby?" Her eyes pierced into mine with anger, but had stopped pushing away from me. Moving to my side letting her keep her secret I took what she would give me. I kissed her cheek, pulled her hand to my mouth to kiss that too. We spent the rest of the night, and most of the next day on the couch touching each other tenderly.

Friday I wanted to take her out, but she wanted to stay at the apartment. Matt was going on a date so we stayed home. She explained that she wanted to spend quality time with me and nothing else matter but the time we were getting together. Sunday night my body hurt with need, and from lying around doing hardly anything. A long shower to wash away my need is what I needed the most, but caved to her going first.

Like we had been doing this all our lives we seemed to move in unison. She went to the shower first while I picked up the living room, which took her forever. After my shower I noticed things were put away, but the best part of all Jess laid in my bed waiting for me. If that didn't make a man's dick hard I don't know what would. Avoiding giving her a full view of my needs I turned away from her to get dressed in boxers.

Crawling into bed next to her, "Jess, are you sleeping."

She turned and cuddled into me, "What do you think?"

Her leg slid between mine and traced upward. I gripped her thigh holding her from the surprise that waited if she went any further up, "No, you're not sleeping."

She rolled her eyes, "No! My legs are smooth, and silky."

This woman had no idea what she did to me all the time. I reached down pulling her leg to avoid my growing hard-on. My hand trailed along the softness of the now shaved legs, which caused a twitch in my groin. This put a smile on my face, "Very nice."

She took my hand and pulled it further up her leg.

This is her way of begging for it, "Jess?"

She grinned and nodded.

I glided my hand further to her as she moved closer to me. My heart was racing. How could I do this when it meant so much more to me than what it would be if we did it now? I love her too much.

Restraining her, hovering over her, and holding her down. My erection zeroing in on the warmth of her sweet spot I pleaded, "Jess, if we are going to do this I have conditions."

With a grin she replied, "I knew that was coming." She nibbled on my lip, "Please don't ask me what I have to do. It will ruin my mood."

Now throbbing with need I shook my head.

Untrusting she urged, "What do you want, then?"

"You."

Not getting it at all she questioned, "You said conditions?"

"Yes. Not tonight. Not for our first time together."

She was skeptical, "What are you thinking?"

I rolled to my back pulling her along with me. Raising both my hands to cup her face and stare into those eyes. She needed to understand what I wanted, "You are special, Jess."

Searching my face for understanding she waited for me to explain.

"I want our night to be as special as you are to me. Remember the night we planned to meet at the cabin?"

I could see the sadness coming to her face.

"You were planning on making love to me. I promised your dad that you would have to say you'd marry me. All those times when I stayed away when I should have given into your needs... I wanted to keep my word, but I also wanted to keep you. I want to make it up to you. I want to make it special, a night to remember for the rest of our lives."

Tears had welled up so much that one dropped out landing on my nose. So far so good now the next part, "After school is done I will get the cabin ready and we'll continue that night."

She shook her head and traced her mouth along my chin, "Sooner."

Not the reply I expected, "How soon?"

The grin on her lips pressed against mine as her teeth nibbled, "Now would work."

I shook my head and held her face to mine looking deep in her eyes, "Your two week vacation this summer."

Eyes glaring, another response I didn't expect, "Okay, fine." She kissed my lips quickly and rolled away from me.

Shit, it didn't work. She's supposed to tell me what she was up to, because this would interfere with what she had to do. She's not supposed to be okay with it. I traced my hand down her arm, "Jess?"

"No, you have your stipulations."

I traced my mouth along her shoulder, "Jess, be realistic... when?"

She turned to me and nuzzled in, "Can it be soon, please."

"Friday?"

She moved up to kiss me, "Make sure there's food and water."

Not understanding her logic, "What do we need that for?"

That sexy, seductive grin grew on her face, "I don't plan on letting you leave this room till Sunday morning."

If anything from tonight made me hard as rock it's a tossup if it's the look in her eye, or the suggestion of lasting three days. Trying to disperse the thought, "It doesn't last that long."

She bit her lip, her eyes lit up, and that smirk told me she would make it last that long. Having a hard on, thinking about having sex with Jess, and having her curled up to me with her lips pressing against my shoulder this would be a sleepless night. Her sleepless night would come Friday, because it would be a night to remember.

# 7

It's hard to believe this week went by so smooth. We went to classes, did homework, and cuddled at night. We ate breakfast, lunch, and dinner together. I loved every minute with her and things changed for the better. She's going to agree to marry me when I ask her, but it had to be on or before Friday night.

I had gotten almost everything except for the flowers, so after class on Friday I stopped at her dorm. She didn't let me in and I found that odd, "Jess, what are you doing?"

"Surprise, why what are you doing?"

"Well, there are a few more things I have to get on my way home and I hoped you'd meet me there about 8 pm."

Her eagerness to go along with this set off alarms in my head, but it had to be my nerves. She pushed out of her room to walk with me to my truck. All touchy feely she wrapped herself to my side, running her hand against my abs, her lips pressing under my chin. So turned on, that I'm worried about lasting even 3 minutes alone with her, but I'd try my hardest to make this special.

I left her looking out my rear view mirror. Standing there watching me leave, her eyes so content on me. She'd say yes tonight for sure.

Rushing home I put candles everywhere. The rose petals sprinkled all over the bedroom. As special occasion required a special dress for Jess, so I laid out the one I bought for this night. With her eyes as green as they were I went for the black evening gown. Wondering how she would look in it would be answered tonight. Not wanting to waste time cooking, I had picked up our dinner. Trying to keep Matt away from the apartment didn't work out. He agreed to stay in his room. Tonight it's Jess and me with no interruptions, no distractions, and nothing to stop us from taking that next step. I set the table and put on music. After a shower I put on dress slacks and a dress shirt. I walked through the apartment nervous as all hell and looked out the window to see if she's here yet. Pleased to see her pull in and park. My instincts told me to rush out and meet her, but going for the seductive controlled personality I waited patiently. Uneasy and nervous I opened the door for her. She is too because she wouldn't even meet my gaze. I stopped her, "At any time, Jess, if you change your mind just talk to me."

Her eyes rose to meet mine full of tears. Assuming they were happy tears it filled my heart. It's finally going to happen, Jess would be all mine after tonight. I directed her to the bathroom, "Your dress is on the bed; meet me at the table."

She walked away glancing back to me as she entered the bathroom.

## *Jessica*

I griped the sink to steady myself as my stomach rolled. Saying good bye to my roommates and packing my car turned out to be harder than I thought it would be. I would be on a plane in 36 hours and it kill me, and what it will do to him I had a good idea. Confused about what I wanted more, to give him a night to remember, or just run leaving him without heartache. The mirror showed a pathetic needy girl who didn't understand how that beautiful pure hearted man could love her. Would he love me through this? That's when I decided I would tell him tonight. If he still wanted to be with me than it would be, if not then I had to let him go. Only doing what he wanted I did my hair, make up, and then snuck to the bedroom. He already set it up for our encounter tonight. Rose petals everywhere, candles arranged around the room perfectly, the sheets and bed spread clean and folded back ready to consume us. At the end of the bed a beautiful black dress laid waiting.

I put fancy underwear I picked up for this night but the dress required no bra. I shook my head with disbelief that he got me one like this.

When I walked out he turned to me with his hand on his chest as he gasped. Not waiting at all I walked over to him and into his open arms he whispered into my ear, "You take my breath away."

Guilt washed over me, "Paul, I have to tell you something."

Not wanting to hear me out, he redirected my attention, "Let's have dinner first."

I swallowed and nodded following his lead to the table. He pulled out the chair for me as I looked back at him. I choked up already, how am I going to tell him the emptiness he had nightmares about is going to come back. In less than 36 hours the sadness is going to engulf us. Tears welled in my eyes so I turned to the table. Tonight is going to be the hardest night in my life. He served me food and sat down to eat with me.

There's hardly anything on his plate so I asked, "You're not hungry?"

A lopsided grin grew on his face showcasing that dimple as he replied, "I'm somewhat nervous."

I reached for his hand, "At any time, Paul, if you change your mind just tell me."

He laughed and scooted closer, "I will never change my mind about you."

I sighed and swallowed to keep the lump coming to my throat.

Silence fell over our dinner as we slowly ate. Scenarios ran through my mind of how I'd tell him. So wrapped in my head I didn't notice how quiet he is. Glancing over to see him dazed and off in his own world. I guess we both were.

He took my hand leading me to the living room where we danced slowly body to body. Reaching my arms around his neck I pulled him closer to stare into his eyes. He took me away from the sadness so easily. I forgot what I wanted to tell him because he helped me to believe that we'd stay this way forever. I didn't have a choice about going, but this was unbelievable and perfect. My fingers slid down his shirt to the first button. Searching his eyes for disapproval I undid the first one, then the second continuing until his shirt opened freely. After letting me trail my hands around him and place that kiss to his chest he made his move slowly walking backwards toward the bedroom. We closed the door when we were in his room. He searched my face wondering if I would change my mind. When you enjoy the tender touch of someone you love the only thing you want to do is take things further. He had been good for long enough and I loved him with my whole heart. We made our way to the bed but stopped at the side. His hands moved to unzip me bit by bit with an antagonizing leisureliness. I sighed with a laugh that's when he stopped to gaze into my eyes. Without the smile his dimples gouged his cheeks. After pulling the strap from my shoulder he kissed there with delicacy that sent shivers down my back. Wanting more of this tingling sensation I held his face to me turning my head to give him room on my neck. His hesitation seemed to stop him from continuing. It's the expression that played on his face left me wondering if he's changing his mind. Watching his eyes search the room my stomach did a flip. Tonight, our last chance to be together and he's changing his mind now? As his eyes came back to meet mine they sparkled bright from the light through the window. Or it could be the thought of consummating our love that made them shine like that. With raised eyebrows he confessed, "Candles."

Relief washed over me as my knees went week. Wanting to fall to the bed I refused to let my body cave so easily. When he let go of me I laughed and observed him lighting each candle as he made his way around the room. Taking each other's hands when we met at the side of his bed he confessed, "I really don't know how to make this perfect."

"You just did, Paul." I put my arms around his neck and kissed him in a way that should have curled his toes. His arms wrapped around my waist and held me tight while returning my kisses. When we both stopped kissing we held tight to each other not knowing how to take the next step. Planning it out like this made it uncomfortable and nervous for both of us.

If we're going to get through this tonight something had to change, "Paul, turn around first."

Brown Puppy dog eyes popped out of his head when he pulled away to see my face. That questioning, doubtful face stared at me as his body went rigid.

My voice a little shaky I pleaded, "I am so nervous. Can we crawl in the bed and explore first?"

Though his lips curved into a smile he only kissed my nose before turning around as I asked. I slid the dress off and crawled into the bed covering myself.

"I'm ready, Paul."

Laughing with anticipation he turned but motioned for me to turn away, "Your turn."

The bed caved under his weight, and the heat of his body warmed me as he crawled in next to me. Not wanting to wait a minute longer to be next to him I curled my body to his. Entwining my legs in his, I ran my hand along his chest, and kissed him over and over along his neck.

He kissed me carefully, but his hand trace up my leg. When his hand reached my core he stopped kissing me, "Did you change your mind?"

I shook my head grinning from ear to ear, "I have never gone to bed completely naked. It's weird."

Again he kissed my nose, but disappeared beneath the covers. Just to witness him in play I lifted the covers. Those eyes came back to meet mine filled with delight. The flick of his tongue against his lips caused a heat reaction between my legs. We would have no problem if he slid into me right now the moisture between my legs told me this. With the sexiest smile on his lips he made contact with my stomach. Instinctively my hand moved to his head running my fingers through his messy hair. A whimper came from deep within me; the sensation too good to refuse. Abruptly it came to an end when he slid my underpants from my body moving away from me further into the depths of the covers. It wasn't in me to complain, but I groaned with disappointment. Crawling back up the bed to me he hovered gazing into my eyes. His stare as innocent as a new born, guilt washed over me for what I have planned.

Voice gruff with restraint he demanded, "Jess, touch me."

Letting my fingers trail up his arms and biceps my attention on how dark his eyes seemed to be getting. Shaking his head he growled out, "Not there Jess."

This is my play time too. Stubborn to give into him I ran my hands up over his shoulders down to his chest only to brush his nipples with the palm of my hands.

Strain filled Paul's face when he closed his eyes and groaned, "Are you teasing me?"

Reaching up I nipped one of his nipples with my teeth.

The warmth of him as he ground his hips against mine sent a thrilling shiver up my spine. Gasping at the sensation only to have it end when he moved to lie down next to me. He propped his head on his hand so that he can look down at me. Hoping it's not over, my eyes wide with wonder why he stopped.

## *Paul*

To keep her legs parted I laid mine between hers. The last thing I wanted her to do is change her mind, but I almost blew when she tried to take a bite out of me. If she wanted to play I would give her what she wanted. After tonight she won't want anyone else for the rest of her life, she's going to be all mine.

Her wide eye stare made me smile, her innocence written on every inch of her face. How she didn't see it on mine I have no idea, but we're going to experience this together

Trailing my fingers against her waist I asked, "Are you afraid to touch me?"

Shock is the only word to explain the expression on her face.

"NO!"

Not the response I expected her to give me.

"Then touch me."

Really trying hard to hold back the grin spreading across my face it's impossible she lit my whole world. When she finally reached to touch me she placed her hand on my face. Her finger traced my dimple as always.

Shaking my head, even chuckling a little I took her hand and brought it to my mouth, kissing her open palm. Taking each finger in my mouth one by one, sucking, licking, and kissing each of them. Coming up with a way to experience this together she had to get over her fear of touching me right now. That is something I would want her to do on a regular basis. Her chest rose and fell rapidly, and all I wanted to do is dive deep into her, but I also wanted her to be completely comfortable with our sexuality together. Leaning away from her, taking her hand down to me, I wrapped her fingers around me. Her lip twitched nervously as I stroked myself with her hand. Releasing her hand from my grip I hoped she would take over handling me.

Her whisper came, "It's hard and soft at the same time."

Moving as close as possible to let her explore my penis, I decided to explore her. She has never been heavily endowed in the breast area, but seeing them now. How perfectly round they are, how fare the skin on her breast is, and the way her nipples puckered there right in front of me. Perfection is what I saw in her. As I ran my finger against the areola she stroked her hand against me. Gently squeezing her nipple between my fingers and then rolling it, she squeezed and stroked harder. The more pleasure she experienced the more she gave me the pleasure of her hand. When her finger rubbed against the tip to find moisture she gasped. Consuming her gasp I took advantage of her mouth. If kissing her wasn't heavenly enough her hand continued to touch, stroke, and message my membrane. If I didn't stop her soon it would be over before it begins. I pulled gently away from her grasp moving down to take each breast in my mouth. I wanted to touch and taste every inch of her. Her protest will come eventually, but for now she let me do what I wanted. Taking her breast in my mouth licking, sucking and nibbling, my reward her hand cupped my head against her. After moving to the other her lips pressed to my forehead with a moan, "Oh Paul!"

To me that's permission to continue, which I had every intention of doing. The end goal to have the warmth wetness of her stroking against me while screaming my name helped me to control the eagerness. I definitely had this in the bag if she already called out my name. Now it's time to get serious. I pulled myself from her grip and slowly kissed her down the middle as I made my way south. Only pausing at her belly button to drive her a little mad as I devoured her there. Both of her hands gripped my hair. Not wanting to wait another second to see her next reaction I made my way to the sweetness of her core and planted a full open mouth kiss.

Pushing up to her elbows looking down at me with an uncertain expressing showing her disbelief of what I just did she scolded, "What are you doing?"

Acting like the devil himself I dipped down only to run my tongue from her opening all the way to her clit keeping my eyes on her for the reaction. Dropping her head back, falling to her back, her hands fisted the sheets when I licked up her clit to suck her flavors. Naturally her legs opened to me as she raised her knees placing her feet to the bed she bucked upward at the sensation. Needing to control her I wrapped my arms around her legs pressing her stomach down as I devoured her into ecstasy. Her whimpers, her cry's, and her moans all came out with my name on the end.

"Paul, I need you now."

Not yet baby, which I didn't take time to tell her. I continue my assault of the wet folds, her clit, and the core of her until her legs shook from pleasure. Slowly I crawled up her as the rest of her body trembled against mine. She's mine all mine, all she has to do is say it.

My own pain of throbbing needed to be satisfied, but I had to hear the words. "Are you sure you want to do this?"

Her word came out breathy, "Yes."

Spreading her wide beneath me I rubbed against her core, "Tell me."

The need in her voice came out pleading, "Please Paul. I need you in me."

I wanted to stay true to my promise to her father. Still not the words I wanted to hear from her I asked, "Are you going to marry me?"

# *Jessica*

Why did he have to make me come if he didn't intend on finishing the job without telling him I would marry him?

He reached between us stroking me with his penis held in his hand. He knew what he was doing and it drove me crazy. Wanting him to fill me with his love before I explained the bomb I intended on dropping on him. Reaching my arms around him to pull him tighter, hoping he wouldn't be able to resist. Taking the tip his penis and placed it against my opening without inserting he drove me mad.

That crazy devil grin came to his face as the pressure of him told me he is there and willing if I said the words. If I told him no, would he stop making love to me? Finally breaking the silence he pushed, "Jessica, you have to tell me you will marry me."

I bit my lip and dug my fingers into his butt pulling him to me, "Not yet, Paul, please."

He took my hand and sucked on my ring finger searching for something with his other hand. When he found what he reached for he slid his mouth from my finger. He gazed at me with pleading eyes as he pushed a little further into me, driving me to want to beg him to do it. I wanted to tell him I'm leaving and that he had to hurry, our time was limited. He slid the ring on my finger, "Please tell me you will marry me?" He pushed into me a little more and I gasp, "A year."

He pushed harder almost in me.

"We can plan on a year?"

"Start planning in a year."

He pushed into me as the tears escaped my eyes and trickled down the side of my face. Waiting to see if it hurt being the first time for me his hands came to hold my face, "Does it hurt?"

I shook my head because it didn't hurt, but my heart did. He pushed to me again as his mouth came to mine deeply. His tongue taunted me as he pushed to me again driving deeper with each stroke. He moaned as he moved to and from me. When he would pull away I wanted to beg him to push into me again, but by the time I would open my mouth he'd dive back into me. Words escaped from him with his mouth on mine, "So warm."

Yes, it's warm, filling, and oddly good to me. His movements became faster as he moaned more. The tingling started in my toes and I gripped him tightly, but his release filled me as his body fell onto mine resting there. His face came to my neck as he kissed, licked, and sucked. I laid there realizing he's done. I traced my hands up and down his back wanting him to move to me more. His lips came to my ear, "You didn't come again did you?"

I smiled and turned my face to kiss him, "It's good."

He laughed with a sigh, "It's not supposed to be good."

I grinned as his face came to mine and he moved a little. I raised my eyebrows as he slipped away from me. We both giggled and kissed more as his body move to mine again. His kisses still filled with need as our mouths moved together. The tingling came back as he swelled inside of me. I had to quit kissing him to breath and his hands came to my face to hold me to look at him as he stroked deeper and deeper. The slower and deeper he went the tingling sensation increased. I gasped and moaned a little. The sound surprised me that it came from me and I closed my eyes with embarrassment. His lips pressed against mine, "There, Jess." diving deep hitting an area inside me that ignited with each stroke. His rhythm easy to follow only increased my longing to have him in every way. I nodded and gasped again. Oh shit that noise escaped from chest this time. His smile grazed my face as he concentrated more on moving the way that was making me moan in ecstasy. Seeing the creases in his forehead grew with his concentration as he moved to me more determined.

It became too intense, "Paul, stop."

He stopped pushing so hard but didn't stop moving that way and I held my breath.

Gasping in between long torturous thrusts he blurted, "Are you okay?"

Something seemed to be happening to my body which I couldn't stop so I nodded and shivered. He went back to moving to me smiling as he stared into my eyes, "Jess, it's supposed to be like this."

When he pushed into me so slowly my body took over rising to meet him, tilting in a way that gave him deeper access to my core. Each movement we made complimented each other as if our bodies took over craving more. The mixed emotions over whelmed us as the tingling moved up my body and festered in my stomach. It's like swinging when you close your eyes and tip back to get that rush of tingling but only better because you had someone to share it with.

Not being able to handle the pleasure tears filled my eyes his voice came deep and careful, "Jess, let it happen, please."

I closed my eyes allowing myself to love him without all the clutter. It became a different world to me as we moved together as one. My movements complimented his as I dug my fingers into his skin. I heard him moan and his body tensed even more. He gasped with every movement into me and I made noises that didn't sound like me at all. He pushed hard to me and this amazing rush filled me causing me to erupt inside and scream out his name. I gasped for air as his movement slowed the pleasure complete. I came with him in me and it was better than I could ever imagine. It wasn't that way the first time, but he didn't stop until I shared that experience with him. I could do that every minute of every day if my body could handle it, only now I'm exhausted and my body limp and weary. If I tried to move it would tremble everywhere. His face rested next to mine his cheek caressing mine. The sensation of his smile glided against my face while whispering, "That is how you make love."

I moaned a yes and kissed his cheek. His mouth came back to mine as we kissed softly, playfully, and loving. His nose nudged mine while our lips consumed each other's. This urge to cry took over causing me to lose it. I couldn't stop the tears from coming and then a sob escaped me. After making love to the man I am madly in love with why would I cry like this? Our love is amazing and wonderful; I never imagined it could be so perfect. I put my arm over my face to hide my embarrassment. I didn't want him to see me this way because I'm not sad at this moment. I am so happy that it filled my heart with everlasting joy.

"Jess, why are you crying?"

I yelled with my squeaky voice, "I don't know."

He laughed slightly but then asked in a serious tone, "Did I hurt you?"

I shook my head and gasped for more air. He moved to hover and I grabbed a hold of him to keep him here.

"What do you want me to do?"

I yelled again this time my voice cracked, "I don't know."

He moved to my side a little and traced his fingers over my face, "You know I love you?"

Still not being able to look at him I nodded.

"Tell me what you are feeling?"

Trembling with my tears I slowly got out, "Scared… Wonderful… Amazing… Happy… Confused."

"Confused?"

"Yeah."

"About me?"

Bellowing, "NO! Why I'm crying."

He laughed and pressed his lips to mine gently, "I heard this could happen."

I lowered my arm to peek at him pleadingly.

"The first time; sometimes it's so emotional when you love someone."

"Great, you could have warned me."

He laughed and kissed my face everywhere, "I love that you are like this. You love me almost as much as I love you."

Pushing him away I tried to roll away from him, but nodded to tell him I did love him as much as he loved me.

Holding me preventing me from escaping his embrace he whispered in my ear, "I have to tell you something."

Pain seared my heart with fear. Did this turn him off? His hand gently pulled my face back to his gazing at me with the softest eyes, "Jess, remember when you wanted me to kiss you?"

Regaining my sanity I nodded, but I sniffled trying to control my tears.

"How you wanted me to be your first for everything?"

I nodded again taking a huge gasp of air and but it came out with quick breaths in, "Yes?"

"You are my first."

Staring into his eyes I couldn't quite get what he said.

"I have never been with anyone but you."

"But, you had lots of girlfriends?"

He grinned, "Because I never wanted to do anything with any of them. You are my first for everything…" He shrugged his shoulders, "Except for kissing."

Still wondering what exactly did he mean, "So, you never did this before with anyone?"

He shook his head as he pressed his lips to mine again. I wrapped my arms around his neck and then my legs. He pulled me close and rolled to his back with me laying on him. I moved down and laid my head on his chest. His kiss came to my head and the trace of his hand down my back comforted me.

We must have laid there for a long time and I rolled from him grabbing the sheet to pull around me. He pulled back on them, "Hey."

I pulled harder and ran to the door.

Reminding me he blurted out, "Matt is out there."

I laughed but still snuck into the bathroom. Pulling the sheet up to use the toilet the surprise came when I stood realizing the toilet filled with redness. With hands trembling I cleaning myself with toilet paper and water, trying to rid myself from the blood that came from me. I had no idea there would be so much from the first time. In a daze moving from the bathroom to his bedroom not knowing how or what I would say to him. As I got closer to him lying there naked, every part of his body ripped in muscles proving how perfect he is. I definitely did not compare. I sat down on the bed not saying a word. His arm wrapped around me and pulled me back to him. He traced his hand down my back lowering the sheet from me, "I wish you wouldn't cover your body. You are the most beautiful person I know."

Not feeling very pretty right now I pushed him away. Evaluating the situation he scooted up against the headboard and reached to pull me to him. He cradled me against his chest, and I couldn't refuse how amazing it felt to have his arms around me. Wrapping my arm around his waist and rested my head to his chest completely curled into him.

His chest rose slowly and sank as air escaped his chest when he asked, "What's wrong?"

A little embarrassed for yelling at him about this very thing a long time ago, it's going to be a hard one to explain.

"Remember that time in your truck when we were messing around."

The squeeze of his embrace came with a laugh as he said, "I remember lots of times when we messed around in my truck."

Frustrated I huffed, "The time I yelled at you because you fingered me."

He pressed his lips to the top of my head, "Yes. You thought I broke your cherry and you didn't want to lose it to fingers." Laughter escaped him as he remembered the scene.

This didn't make me happy, so I reached up pulling his face to look at me, "I didn't"

Laughter still filled his eyes, "Of course you didn't"

Raising my eyebrows hinting at the situation.

"Oh..." He breathed out as the realization came to him. He pushed me forward, rearranged the pillows, gently laid me down on the bed. When I was all tucked in he laid next to me propping his head in his hand to gaze at me. His hand gently rubbed my stomach, "Are you in any pain?"

More embarrassed than experiencing any pain I shook my head no. Closing my eyes his hand left my stomach only to touch my face gently as he traced the contours of it.

Relaxing with his soft touch luring me into sleep I closed my eyes to enjoy the intimacy of his tenderness.

# 8

I woke to the most amazing sensation of a large tender hand tracing down my back and a warm breeze on my neck with the faintest touch to my ear. I didn't move so that he would continue to touch me this way. The curve of his body against mine burned my skin. His chest pressed against my shoulder when he leaned over to kiss my back gently. Flipping his hand over; he ran his fingers down the middle of my back slowly. Once he got to my lower back his thumb moved back and forth across my lower back. Easing his touch I barely felt his hand against my skin as it skimmed over my butt causing a great big grin to fill my face. The hardness of his erection rubbed against me and a moan of need escaped his chest. As he touched me, running his hand down my leg, he pulled it up a little while his breathe became heavy. He moved to hover over me lowering himself so his shaft rubbed against my wet folds enticing me to wake from this perfect dream. When his mouth came to my shoulder blades he kept his mouth open as he traced my back gently gliding his lips over my skin. He rubbed against me again and my craving to have him in me increased. Caving to that need I rolled over facing him. The grin on his face grew showing those dimples that lured me to his face. Reaching for him when he decided to move away from me I gave him the pout. Scooping up the rose petals he tossed them in the air allowing them to fall all over. As his eyes roamed over my body his thoughts showed on his face with that crooked mischievous grin appearing on his perfect mouth. Working his way up my body slowly blowing the petals away from my skin he placed butterfly kisses to my body inch by inch. Twisting, turning, curving, and arching, my body craved the attention. It was the tip of his tongue to my abdomen that made me squeak out my pleasure. My toes tingled, my core wet and ready, all he had to do would be to slide into me, but he didn't. He sat back on his heals admiring the sight laid out in front of him. I am putty in his hands.

His fingers and hands wrapped around my wrists as he pulled me up into his lap, until his arm wrapped around my waist holding me to him. Lost in the depths of his eyes as they lingered on mine I'd agree to do anything he wanted right now all he'd have to do is ask. My legs wrapped around his waist as I waited for the new experience he'd bring me.

Pressing his forehead to mine he breathed in deeply let out the words with the release of his lungs, "I have never wanted anyone or anything more than you at this very moment." Reaching around his neck to pull him closer to me even one inch between us is too far apart. Holding me away from his body long enough to allow the hardness of his erection to easily penetrate my sweet spot, diving deep into my soul. Wetness of his mouth attacked my breasts licking sucking and nipping himself into a frenzy as his body rocked into mine. His thrust came deeper, harder than I expected. When his eyes fell on mine I wasn't surprised how dark they had become. Possession of greed filled him as his body rocked eagerly to me. Too fast for me or my liking I whispered, "Slower."

Instant conflict filled his face. My needs verse his. Gliding my hands down his back I noticed every muscle tensed at my touch as he slowed down his movements for me. The strength in his arms held me while the slowness of his invasion reached the spot of sensation I needed and wanted. Allowing myself to get lost a deep moan came from deep within me without my control. The intensity of his thrusts increased again, but it caused the loss of the pleasure I'm so close to having. This time I ordered him, "Slower!"

A growl escaped him, "Jess, I can't." His body moved faster again. I kissed everywhere and mouthed to him, "Oh, Paul. Please slower."

I tried to kiss him he turned his head to concentrate on his movements, every thrust straining his body beyond any pleasure. So close to release, another gasping moan came from me, and he moved even slower. Pulling almost all the way out and slowly inserting until he hit my inner core. After the fifth or sixth time he spoke into my ear, "Come on baby. I need you to come, NOW!"

His demand triggered my body to respond gasping out, "Yes, Paul. Oh yes. Oh Paul. Yes." Craving this new pleasure I wanted more. Releasing Paul from agony I begged, "Paul, harder!"

Holding me tighter to his body every muscle bulging he gasped into my ear, "You sure?"

I wanted him hard and fast my need out weighting my thoughts, "Yes."

His smile pressed against my cheek still not giving me what I wanted he replied, "You're positive?"

"YES."

My body already in motion to be pressed against the bed before I got the full word out, and yes is a short word. My legs propped over his biceps tipping my body up to him. The position a little uncomfortable until he circled his hips with each trust causing his hardness to stroke things within me I had no idea they existed. Yelling out in bliss, "Yes baby!" seemed to encourage him more. In with a swerve of his hips, and retreat that left me wanting more, the deep dive into me and the speed all too much at one time. Fisting my hands in the sheets was all I could do to hold on to my sanity. Lost in the intensity of it all; Paul glorious in his demands, "That's it baby. Come for me again. Come for me hard!" When I opened my eyes again the triumph showed on his face; the proudness of giving me pleasure evident as he ground into me deeply and thoroughly. Leaning down to kiss me he spoke into my mouth, "That's it baby. Tell me how much you like it."

Heat sprayed into me as I screamed out Paul's name over and over again until I had nothing left to say. He's a god in bed and he is mine to have.

When he rolled over so fast I thought something was wrong. He released his hold on my legs and my body rested on his with the warmth of him still lodged between my legs. I was afraid to move, because if he wasn't in me I would be empty. We fell back to sleep in each other's arms.

I woke and kissed him where my mouth had been resting on him. His chest so beautifully cut and I loved to touch every curve of his body. He sighed, "I am starving."

Laughing I reminded him, "I told you to bring food."

"I didn't think we would stay in here this long."

I crawled over top of him, "We have been waiting a long time for this."

He smiled and traced his hands up my sides pulling me to him, "Was it worth the wait?"

Kissing him softly, and then I rolled my eyes gesturing that I had to think about it. His irritation that I didn't reply right away boiled over as he grabbed me and rolled over on top of me, "Are you teasing me?"

"Yes, Paul. You were worth the wait." I kissed his cheek, "Am I?"

His kiss came hard and passionate as he mouthed to me, "Oh, yes...yes...yes."

I laughed and pushed him away, "Food, Paul. I am hungry."

He laughed and traced his hand against me, "You want more?"

"No, and I am sore so no more of that today."

He frowned at me, "Really?"

Nodding with my response, "Yeah, really sore now."

He laughed, "Wow. I didn't realize you'd get sore."

I touched his penis, "You're not?"

He pulled away, "Yeah, but that is because I do all the work."

I pushed him away and he grabbed his boxers trying to slide them on and almost fell over but grabbed the bed just in time. I laughed at him grabbing the sheets pulling them over me. He crawled back up to me, "Jess, one thing."

"What's that?"

He grinned and bit my lip, "Don't freak out but we are getting married."

I put my hand on his face and pushed him away.  He laughed and went out of the room but taking one last glimpse at me.

I rolled over curling up with a pillow and admiring the ring that's on my finger, torn between smiling and the sadness.  Would he understand that I have no choice, and would he wait for me?  I do love him and I want to marry this beautiful, hunky, muscular man.

Would it be easier if he thought I didn't love him?  Would he be able to breathe if I convinced him it's completely over this time?  No matter what I would do he's going to get hurt and I love him so much.

"Jess, are you sleeping?"

Turning to watch him walk back into the bedroom, his face full of concern; I must have let the sadness take over.  He moved to the bed with a tray of food, but stared at my eyes with wonder.  It took everything in me to give him a little smile as I thought about being away from him in less than 18 hours.  He set the tray down on the night stand and crawled over to me, "Jess, don't do this.  Don't be scared.  Please, just trust that I love you and we won't plan anything for a year."

I touched his face as the tears in my eyes leaked out.  I gave him a better smile this time, but his loss of understanding left him speechless.

He grabbed the food and gave me a forkful of scrambled eggs.  We devoured the whole plate and he fed me grapes as I curled up in his arms and rested on his chest.

We only ventured out for the bathroom use.  I brushed my teeth and took a shower, but went back to him as quickly as possible.  He took a turn but his showers took too long for me.  He didn't understand that we didn't have much time left.  I walked in and tried to hurry him.  He just laughed at me and took his time.

"If you miss me this much come in here."

I peeked in and shook my head, "Still sore."

He laughed and continued.  I gave up and went back to bed to wait for him.  When he finally returned I curled into him again and traced my hands over his body.  I wanted to get my fill so that I'd survive this journey I had to take.  Just holding him next to me gave me too much time to think about leaving.  Fear kept me from telling him even though I wanted to spill everything.  After all this time we finally connected and he'd refuse to let me go.

As the time ran out I tried to plot out how I'd do this, but every time I try to get up he wakes.  Asking myself, *"How am I going to get out of here?"*  I needed to get rid of the pictures on his computer so he wouldn't have to be reminded of me during my absence.  With the intention of keep the pain to a minimum; I would leave a note.  What should I say?  I love you but goodbye?  No, I wanted him to wait for me.  Torn between leaving the pictures and telling him I had to leave for a year, or leaving them so he'd remember me.

He was distracting me with his hands as they glided over my skin. He brought me back to this moment and I gazed up at him. The smile on his face was completely adorable. I nuzzled back into him and he sighed with pleasure.

When it was getting late and the sun was going down my heart filled with pain as it thudded against my chest. He took it the wrong way and decided to be playful again.

I insisted, "No! More food."

He grunted as he moved from the bed and went to the kitchen. This time I followed wrapped in the sheet. He peeked back at me concerned, "Jess, I'll bring it to you."

I walked over to him and wrapped my arms and the sheet around him resting my head to his back. His hand reached around me holding my lower back to pull me closer. I kissed him and kissed him. He finally turned around and put something in my mouth; it tasted amazing.

He pulled me to the table and I sat on the table facing him in the chair as we ate. They were little sandwiches but in a flower tortilla all rolled together. We laughed and giggled as we ate the whole plateful. Matt walked in, "What are you two doing out of the room? I didn't think you'd surface until Monday."

We both laughed but Paul answered, "Yeah, we do have to eat."

"You guys are having sex and she is sitting on our table. I eat there."

I giggled, "But I have a sheet wrapped around me."

He shook his head, "Yeah, in the sheets you had sex in. Jess, that is disgusting."

"Matt, settle. The table can be washed."

Paul pulled me to him, "We should go back to the room so we don't gross Matt out anymore."

He lifted me and headed for the room. I made him stop for brushing again. We stood there together as his body grazed mine. We giggled and watched each other in the mirror until we finished. As we went from the bathroom to the bedroom we heard Matt yell, "You didn't do it in there; did you?"

We laughed moving into his room but Paul answered, "No, you're safe to use the bathroom."

In a rush to get back in bed he pulled his boxers off and laid down gesturing me to come lay with him. I wanted him to be so tired that he wouldn't wake when I left. It would hurt too much to see his face. I crawled over him pulling up the sheet as I sat on him. He looked up at me his eyebrows up with wonder. I rubbed against him.

"What are you doing?"

"You do all the work!" I gave him a look that would challenge him to not move at all.

He grinned, "Okay I won't do anything. It's all you this time."

Winning the argument I grinned and rubbed against him more. It wasn't long before he closed his eyes allowing the sensation take over, growing long, hard, and willing under me. Maneuvering my body to find the right spot his hands came to my thighs gripping.

"Paul!"

He moved his hands away from me putting them behind his head. That crooked smile stayed on his face even though his eyes closed. When I pushed to him a little the smile went away and his face changed from happy to pain.

"Does it hurt?"

He shook his head as the smile came back. I pushed a little more and he slid into me easily. His eyebrows furrowed and a grimace came back to his face. Forcing himself to stay calm and relaxed with long slow breathes. Using his abs as leverage I push away from him all the way to the tip of his erection only to slowly consume him again. His mouth opened and a sound from deep in his chest came out in a low moan. Continuing the agonizing slowness the agony came and went from his face. When his hands came back to grip my thighs he growled, "Oh, shit Jess."

Controlling him I scolded once again, "Paul!" Easing up a little I allowed his hands to stay on me but shifted my hips as my body consumed him again. Explaining the movement, "This is how to go slow."

His hands moved away from me but gripped the head board and his hips raised to thrust into me prematurely. Happiness filled my heart that he wanted me badly and this drove him mad. Reminding him once again I deepened my voice, "Paul!"

He moaned with dislike but lowered as I pushed harder to him.

"Oh, Jess." His eyes opened full of need, only to close again as I gave him what he needed with a harder faster rock against him. When his eyes scrunched in the effort to control the release his body so badly needed the moans and verbal pleas became constant. Giving in to him I gave everything I had moving faster and harder until surly he couldn't stop himself, and then I slowed back to a snail's pace.

"No... no... no... please... no."

When I pushed to him he released the head board sitting up pulling me to him. The need of our bodies took over enhancing every movement, every breath, and every heartbeat. Starting where we connected our bodies enveloped each other.

Even after the heat of his release scorched my inside bursting my release, he continued to move in me. Hard and full in length his coming didn't satisfy his craving. Leaning back bracing myself as he worked hard to get himself off, but nothing seemed to be enough.

As he slid away from me I worried that he had given up on the second release of the moment. That the intensity of this too much to handle.

When I felt his arms link under my legs I understood. He pinned me to a better angle for his rough thrust. No matter how many times I came, he always had more for me if I wanted.

The pleasure of us together unexplainable, but not enough to satisfy the hunger of more, and I wanted more of him. The slight kisses to every part of our bodies as we made love. It didn't matter where our mouths were because we kissed whatever part of the body that's there for the taking. The exploration of our touching of our hands enhanced the desires we experienced. I wanted him to know I loved every part of him and every part of us being together.

He finally rolled to his back completely exhausted, "I don't know where you came from, but oh my god do I love this." I reached back and propped up the pillows and moved to lean back. He rolled to me resting his head on my stomach. His hands and arms reached around me to hold me. I could watch him for eternity never getting tired of watching him fall to sleep. The pain in my heart came back at the thought of my departure. Running my fingers through his hair while my mind ran wild with worry for what this would do to him.

Hoping exhaustion would keep him sleeping, I tucked a pillow under his head as I inched my way from him. When his arm wrapped around me tighter I rubbed his back until the tension in his arm relaxed again.

After getting out from under him I whispered his name, "Paul?" to see if he'd answer. With no response I made my way to the computer where I inserted the disk to download the pictures on it. Tears pricked in my eyes when I deleted them from his computer. Knowing I'd hurt him when I left, this would hurt him even more. The only reason I had to do this was to keep it from reminding him of me. He had to live his life while I'm away. Not look at me on a daily basis to only feel that pain over and over again.

"Jess, what are you doing?"

Jumping at the sound I went into panic mode, "I have to start a new job in the morning. Just checking what time I have to be there."

He held out his hand for me and I got up taking it and crawling back in with him. I traced my fingers through his hair and rubbed his back.

"Is this part of the thing that you have to do but don't want to talk about?"

I whispered, "Yes."

"If it's a new job are you staying up here for summer, because we could live here? You could move your stuff in and I could stay here with you and wait for you to get done. I could feed you and you know. We could be together."

I wanted to stay here with him so badly, but that wasn't going to happen. I rubbed his back more, "I would love that Paul."

He kissed my stomach and put his head back down on my belly. I waited for him to sleep again and then I moved out from under him yet again. I went to his desk to write the note, but had no idea of what to say to him.

*Dear Paul:*

*I cannot explain the love I feel for you. This has been the best days of my life and I will cherish them forever.*

*What I am regretting is the months ahead. You see when I was miserable I agreed to do something that would take me away from you. I didn't know how to tell you or what to tell you. I tried to stay away, but you are so darn cute. Your persistence caught me unprepared to keep you away and now that we have had our moment I don't want to leave. But the choice and the commitment already made.*

Glancing back at him the tears began to fall. No matter what I agreed to in my heart I didn't want to leave him. Not now or ever. Letting my eyes fall to the ring on my hand as the tears streamed down my face. This pain will be unbearable for both of us. I wiped my face and tried to continue.

*I tried to figure a way to cause less pain, but the pain will come. I deleted the pictures of me so that you would not have to be reminded of me every day. I am leaving your ring with hopes that someday you will forgive me and place it on my finger again. I am not allowed to bring things of value so the phone is yours too.*

*If you find it in your heart to forgive me someday I would love another chance to spend my life with you. Until then I don't have a choice.*

*I'll be gone one year, but I tried to make it easy for you. There is nothing left of us together except for the memory in our brains. The initial pain last about six months Paul and if you can survive that the pain will lessen.*

*As far as where I am going. Well, at the time I needed to find a place where the pain was greater than my own from missing you. I found it! And now the pain of being away from you will engulf me once again*

My tears dripped on the paper and I wiped them away but it smeared the paper a little. Taking my last fill I looked back at him and gasped from my pain.

*I am sorry, Paul. For leaving, for not being able to face you and most of all for the pain that is to come. I think you feel the same as me and I know I will walk in darkness for the next year.*

*I love you!!!!!!!!*

*Jessica*

Getting up I folded the note grabbed my stuff, and stood over him regretting having to leave. I wanted so much to touch him and hold him one last time but the pain would be too much. If he woke up I wouldn't be able to conceal the pain in my heart. I went to the bathroom to get dressed and washed my face to compose myself.

I walked out putting the note, ring, and cell phone on the table.

"Jess, what are you doing?"

My heart dropped when I heard Matt. I closed my eyes not turning to him and I tried to get the words out with a normal tone but I knew my voice was going to betray me.

"Um, I start a new job this morning and I have to go."

He was walking towards me, "Why are those things on the table?"

Caught in the act of hurting Paul again I didn't want to face him I turned and sprinted to hug him tight.

"Jess, you are scaring me. You should let me wake Paul."

Not letting that happen I shook my head and looked up at him full of tears. Nothing I did could hold in the hurt I already felt. Not only having trouble breathing but to swallow, impossible due to the lump in it. Gasping I blubbered, "Matt, you don't want to do that. Um, I left him a note and it will be okay. Just make sure that he knows I love him with my whole heart. And you need to be there for him. Don't let him do anything harmful to himself."

"Jess, tell me what is going on?"

"Promise me right now! You won't let him hurt himself. I need him."

"Of course not, Jess, but what are you doing?"

Convincing myself this would be the best way for Paul I forced a smile on my face and kissed his cheek. I knew he would wake Paul as soon as I made it out of the door.

He held me tight not letting go, "Jess, where are you going?"

Not giving a true answer I replied, "Where the pain is greater than Paul's and mine."

When I pushed myself from him I put my hand on the note, "Make sure he gets this, will you?"

"Jess, tell me what is happening here?"

Having the best and worst day in my life all wrapped into one day I headed for the door. There's one thing that Matt needed to understand so Paul would; that I would be back. Letting the tears fall I glanced back with only one thing left to say, "Take care of him until I come back please. I love him."

Closing the door I ran to my car. It would have to be a quick getaway. Driving away with my eyes on the rear view mirror seeing Paul run out of the door with his hands entangled in his hair retched at my heart. He didn't understand why I would do this, and he would never understand that I didn't have a choice.

# 9

## *Paul*

I woke to Matt having a panic attack, "Paul, get up Jess is leaving."

"Yeah, she is starting a new job this morning."

He tossed me my boxers and pulled me off the bed, "No, it's more than that."

Confused with his frantic voice and his determination to get me up, "What are you talking about?"

"You better hurry or you won't be able to stop her from leaving."

"I need to stop her?"

"She left the ring, her cell phone, and a note."

I jumped up, "She left the ring?"

He moved to the window allowing me to get dressed, "Yes, damn it. Hurry up. Shit, she started her car, Paul."

I got up and ran out to watch her drive away. I ran back inside going up the steps two at a time. Storming in the apartment and advancing on Matt, "What did she say?"

"She was crying, Paul, and mumbling something about pain being worse than yours and hers."

Not registering everything that just happened I picked up the ring and slid it on my pinky and opened the note.

*Dear Paul:*

*I cannot explain the love that fills my heart when you're in it. This has been the best days of my life and I will cherish them forever.*

My voice firm and angry I let out my comment, "Then why the fuck did you leave the ring?"

*What I am regretting is the months ahead. When I was miserable I agreed to do something that would take me away from you.*

Shaking my head I realized I should have been more insistent on finding out what she had to do, especially if we had to be apart for it.

*I didn't know how to tell you or what to tell you. I tried to stay away, but you are so darn cute. Your persistence caught me unprepared to keep you away and now that we had our moment I don't want to leave.*

Glancing up at Matt for answers only to see him wipe his face with his hands; he is as upset by this as me. So I'm not over reacting because this confuses me. I closed my eyes voicing my opinion, "If you didn't want to leave, why didn't you tell me? Fuck Jessica!"

*But the choice and the commitment had already taken place.*

Shaking my head not believing this happened. She had to at least tell me where she's going. I continued to read.

*I tried to figure a way to cause less pain, but the pain will come. I deleted the pictures of me so that you wouldn't be reminded every day. Also I am leaving your ring with hopes that someday you will forgive me and place it on my finger again. Valuables are not allowed so the phone is yours too.*

Broken is a better word for what this did to me. Walking in my room going to my computer I clicked on my photos, but they're gone just like she said.

Matt followed, "What? Did she leave you the address, a map, WHAT?"

Choking back the bile that worked its way up from my stomach the only thing I could get out, "My pictures of her..." The emptiness filled me from the inside out. Grabbing the desk to hold myself up I raised the letter to continue to read.

*If you find it in your heart to forgive me someday I'd love another chance to spend my life with you. Until then I don't have a choice.*

Blinking away the tears in my eyes I argued with the letter, "Yes, you did have a choice! Damn it! I'd done anything to help you to help keep you here. Why didn't you see that?"

Matt walked over to me staring at me. Not able to take my eyes from the letter I continued to read.

*I'll be gone one year, but I tried to make it easy for you. There is nothing left of us together except for the memory in our brains. The initial pain last six months Paul and if you can survive that the pain will lessen.*

The sound of my sorrow came out in a groan, "No Jess. This can't be happening, you didn't need to leave. A fucking year!"
Matt voice cracked, "A Year?"
Completely devastated I held up the letter yelling at Matt, "That's what it says!"
He shook his head in disbelief as I continued to read.

*As far as where I am going? Well, at the time I needed to find a place where the pain was greater than my own from missing you. I found it! And now the pain of being away from you will engulf me once again*

I fell to my knees to pray that this wasn't happening. My body grew numb: it felt the same as the day Anne died right in front of me.

*I am sorry, Paul. For leaving, for not being able to face you and most of all for the pain that is to come. Understanding what we mean to each other I am sure I will not be the only one walking in darkness for the next year.*

A sob escaped me when I realized that she's right I will walk in total darkness for the next year. Going into autopilot I got up even though my entire body shook from the adrenaline trying to pump life back into my veins. I had to stop her, there had to be a clue, a way to stop her, a way prevent this torture.

Glancing at Matt for answers, but his face filled with pity. The day my parents brought me to the psychiatrists Matt had that hopeless look on his face. He put out his hand for the note so I handed it over to him with hope that he would find a clue of how to stop her from leaving.
Rushing around my room I grabbed a few things shoving them into a bag then headed towards the door. Matt yelled from my room, "Oh my god, Paul. What happened?"
I had no idea what happened. Why she'd leave after agreeing to marry me. I ran out the door, "I need to stop her."

He followed right out the door, stopping for a second to check that the doors locked, "How? We don't know where she is going."

Starting with the most obvious I confirmed, "Her dorm."

This time I didn't argue that he wanted to drive. Lost in my own head with the idea of not seeing her for a year I couldn't see the road threw the tears. He drove fast to the dorm making me thankful. I ran up to her room and knocked frantically. Karlie answered the door sleepily, "Paul, Matt, what are you doing here?"

"Is Jess here?"

"No, she packed all her stuff on Friday and didn't plan on coming back. She's supposed to be with you."

I shook my head, "Did she say where she's going?"

"No. She had personal issues and that's when I noticed her hanging out with Iaesha."

"Who is Iaesha?"

"This strange girl that's into volunteering to help people in troubled countries."

A cool sensation moved through my body as I realized she's leaving, leaving. More like far away from me. If I wanted to change this outcome I had to get to her before she left, "Where is Iaesha's dorm?"

Karlie grabbed a robe and joined my pursuit down the stairs. We knocked and knocked and finally someone came to the door, "What is it?"

Karlie addressed her, "What are you doing here?"

"What do you mean? I go to school here."

"Where is Jessica?"

"She has to be on a flight this morning."

This nightmare got worse and worse. Blood rushed to my hands, which grew into fists. I wanted to hit this girl in the face but Karlie prodded more, "I thought you were going with Jess."

"No, I'm not going. I help from here. I get recruits and sign them up to go help."

Anger pounded hard against my head. Moving closer to her, "Where is she going?"

"South America!"

My blood pumped hard in my veins. So close to losing it completely I forced myself to hold it together so I could pry for more info, "Where in South America?"

The glare I got triggered my anger. My hands fisted, but the only movement was my eyebrow with a questioning rise.

She shrugged, "How am I supposed to know? They don't tell me those things."

Having to get away from her before I punched her in the face I took off at a full run. I had to stop her; I had to get to her first.

Karlie yelled after me, "Paul, I'm sorry."

Getting in the truck I ordered Matt, "Go to Jess's house."

"What?"

"Head to her house."

"But... She's not here?"

How do I explain this one, "She thinks she has to go to South America. She signed up for something and she is heading to the airport but I bet she won't leave without saying goodbye to her mom and dad. We'd catch her there."

Thankfully he took off and headed to the cities. Two and a half hour drive of misery, wondering how he would cope without her for a full year. Repeatedly he wished she'd told me about this situation. She says she loves me and she didn't want to leave, but felt helpless. Remembering how I had asked about this without knowing and her avoidance on telling me. After my process of the way things had progressed I yelled out, "Damn it!"

"What?"

I closed my eyes as the pain poured out. The words fell from my mouth, "I sensed she had a problem, but every time I brought it up she'd cry. I didn't want to upset her so I dropped it. I should have..."

"Don't blame yourself, Paul. She has always done things the wrong way. I don't want to sound mean, but she drives you crazy with her ways of manipulating it so that what she thinks is best for you."

"No! I'm wrong. What I did to her over the last few years, wrong. Did she say anything else?"

"Yeah, I am supposed to make sure you don't do anything stupid to yourself. I'm also supposed to take care of you so when she comes back you will still be here."

I shook my head, and held it in my hands, "Please go faster."

He laughed, "Call her dad. Do they know what she is doing?"

"I don't think so." When I pulled out my phone I noticed the ring still on my pinky. With a promise to Jess I kissed it and then dialed Theo.

"Hey kid. It's way too early in the day, so what's up with you?"

"Jess, left."

"What?"

"She is going to South America. Don't let her leave."

"What?"

"If she shows up there don't let her leave."

"Slow down. Explain this to me."

"I'd explain if I…" I started to cry and handed my phone to Matt. Explaining this to Theo I'd have to admit she left me.

I listened to Matt explain everything we learned while I collected myself. When he finished explaining I got on the phone in time to hear him take a deep breath, "Okay son. Just hurry."

I hung up the phone and stared out the window going through everything in my mind. Her face kept reappearing as I watched her smile, her pleasure, and her eyes as the sparkled in the candle light. Everything I researched to make sure she'd never want anyone else to touch her the way I did, and it didn't compare to the real thing. We're perfect together with the pleasure the desires and fitting so right. Why didn't she just tell me right away? I could have stopped this from happening. We're supposed to be planning our future not time apart.

## *Jessica*

As I drove home the tears continued to stream down my face. Short on time I wouldn't be able to argue with mom and dad, so I had to find a ride to the airport to avoid a long explanation. Also if Paul showed up they wouldn't be able to lead him to me

"Jess?"

"Hey, Greg, I need a favor."

"What is up?"

"I need a ride to the airport. Can you meet me at my house at 5:45?"

"Am or pm?"

"Like in a half hour."

"Where are you going?"

"Um, remember how isolated I had been when I broke up with Paul?"

He answered with caution, "Yes."

"Well I decided that I would go somewhere the pain is deeper than my own. I signed up for it last November, but I need a ride to the airport. Can you do it?"

"Yeah, I'll just throw on some clothes. Pick you up in a few."

"Thanks."

I pulled into the driveway and ran inside with my bags. Dad stopped me in the kitchen, "What are you doing home?"

Still full of tears I demanded, "I have to go dad."

As I pushed by him mom stood second in line, "You need to explain what you're doing."

"If only I had time. I'm supposed to be there by 6 am." I pushed by them and they followed. I dug for summer clothes and stuffed them in my bag.

Dad sounded concerned, "Where are you going?"

Stopping for a second I turned to him, "I had to go where the pain is worse than mine, dad. When Paul didn't show up at the cabin I agreed to go and it's like the military. Once you sign up you don't change your mind."

Mom asked, "So you tried to change your mind?"

"Yes. I went to the administration office and talked to someone but they essentially told me I had to go. Because I signed a document before they purchased the airfare it's final. I'm going." Everything that I hoped for lost to this commitment I lost it entirely as the tears streamed out now. Mom and dad eased up on the lecture. In fact they tried to console me but there isn't time for this. I hugged and kissed them both.

Mom cried, "You agreed to marry Paul?"

I nodded while trying to stop crying. Wiping my face swiftly but the tears came faster and harder. I pushed pass them with my bag in hand barking my orders, "I won't be able to call or get in touch with you for the first month. After that I'm not sure how it will work, but I will try as soon as I can. I hugged each of them again and kissed them saying my goodbyes, but looking out the front window I didn't see Greg yet.

The phone rang and dad went to answer it. "Yeah, kid she is here... No, we can't stop her... She tried and it's not possible... Of course I believe her... yes, of course." He held the phone out for me. I shook my head as the tears were flowing harder, "Please, dad I can't."

He held the phone out for me, "You said you would marry him. He deserves an explanation."

Refusing didn't work. Dad raised his eyebrows, "I know what happened between you two."

I grabbed the phone sobbing, "What?"

"Jess, why are you leaving?"

"I don't have... a choice... the day at the admin's... office I asked... you were waiting... I gave into you... I love you..."

"But why did you agree to go?"

"Because you didn't show up at the cabin."

With anger in his voice, "Is this a payback?"

I screamed at him, "No. I love you! There is no choice I'm going. I agreed a long time ago, because my heart hurt."

"Jess, just don't go. We can figure this out."

"Paul, we have to let go now."

I handed the phone back to dad and hastily kissed his cheek again. Moving to mom I hugged and kissed her cheek, "I will get a hold of you as soon as I can."

Dad put the phone to his face again to talk to Paul. Regret and pain filled every part of my body so hearing his voice dug the pain deeper. Letting my dad know I whispered, "I do love him."

I ran out the door to Greg's truck. I through my bags in the truck and got in the front seat. He looked at me and put out his hand for me. I took his hand in mine clasping it tightly and cried my eyes out all the way to the airport. He didn't say a word, because he understood how much I loved Paul.

## Paul

"Theo, don't let her go. Please don't let her leave. I am almost there. I need to understand."

"Paul, she said she tried and they wouldn't let her back out. She is going out the door."

"No, please don't let…"

Grasping for anything I begged, "I'm afraid she won't come back."

"Paul, calm down. Just get here."

I hung up the phone pleading with Matt to go faster. Unlike Matt he drove like a mad man, but she's slipping through my fingers and there's nothing to stop it from happening.

Jumping out of the car as he pulled into the driveway I ran in the house grabbing Theo's shirt begging, "Where did she go?"

"South America."

"No, what airport? I need to stop her."

He grabbed my arms, "You can't stop her. She has to go."

"NO! She is mine now. I'm going to stop her from leaving. She is going to marry me. Theo she said yes!"

Tears blurred my eyesight but I made a mad dash to her room. Digging through her drawers pulling things out letting them clutter the floor, but nothing. Her desk as neat as always only disrupted with my panic shuffling of the papers searching for a clue. The contents of her bag from school dumped on her bed I grabbed and tossed items looking for information. Nothing to be found I made my way outside to her car. Under her seat, in her glove box, and her trunk but not a thing with what airport she's scheduled to depart. She must have left something that would tell me what her flight number is. There was nothing. I ran back in the house but stopped as they waited for my return. The sympathy in their eyes is too hard for me to see, so made my way to her room again. Believing that my efforts are a lost cause, I stared at her room in bewilderment. How did I let this happen, let her lose her control to where she assumed this is her only route? She should have told me what was going on, there had to be a loophole in the document that she signed. My hand found her sweat shirt so I pulled it to my face falling to my knees. Falling to the floor I leaned against her bed putting the sweet shirt to my face. As if smelling her would bring her back to me. The memory of making love to her repeated in my mind. How our love had been so perfect.

"Paul, son, what are you doing?"

I lowered her sweatshirt enough to look at him, "She destroyed everything, all my pictures of us together. She left the ring that I put on her finger last night, and the phone. I can't even call her."

"You gave her a ring?"

"Yes! Damn it. She said yes. She agreed to marry me." I shook my head and put the sweatshirt over my face again.

He came and sat down on the bed putting his hand on my shoulder.

"I waited for her and she waited to be with me. She is the only girl I have ever… We were going to get married."

He put his hand on my shoulder and walked out leaving me here to sulk in my misery. I got a rush of excitement and ran out, "Matt, take me to the airport. I have to find her."

The phone rang and we all turned to it at the same time knowing it would be her. Theo walked over and picked it up saying hello. He looked right at me and held the phone out to me.

Cradling the phone into my neck like it was her I pleaded, "Jess, oh my god. Please tell me where you are, I will come get you?"

"No, Paul, not this time."

"Jess, tell me what I am supposed to do?"

"You need to let me go."

"No! I love you."

"Paul, I've always loved you and I always will. Bye Paul."

"No, please don't hang up, Jess. Just tell me where you are. Why are you doing this?"

"So it will be easier."

"What will be easier? Revenge Jess, for all the times I stood you up?" Lowering my voice I continued to plead, "I told you that I waited for you too. What we shared." What I wanted to talk about couldn't be said aloud with her dad right behind me.

"No. So it will be easier to get through this, because no matter how bad I want to stay with you I can't. I did try Paul, I truly did. You need to let me go now even though I don't want to go."

"Jess, please don't do this."

"Paul, the pain will last six months and then it will fade and you will forget."

"I will never forget you, Jess. I am in love with you and after this weekend how come you didn't tell me about this?"

"Paul, I couldn't stand to see the pain on your face. It would have been harder for me, because I experienced it too, and now it will burn a whole in my heart being away from you."

"I already lost one person that I loved; please don't do this to me."

"I am not doing this to you, Paul. Don't you see I am trying to make it easier for you? I only got rid of the pictures so that you wouldn't be reminded of me over and over again as you viewed them. That's what made it hard for me. I am so sorry for this Paul. I love you."

"Then don't go. I will take care of it."

"You can't. Not this time, Paul. The decision was made back in November."

"When I didn't show up at the cabin on time?"

"Yes."

"Oh, Jess, why didn't you tell me? I would've dropped everything for you."

"But you didn't, Paul. Like always you'd expect me to understand and that is why I expect you to understand this."

"Jess, I had no idea that it was so painful for you. Please tell me where you are going?"

"You are kidding me. You didn't know I was miserable. I begged and pleaded with you to spend time with me. I was dying inside and you continued to keep doing it. I loved you, Paul, more than anything in this world and I still do."

"Jess, please. I am begging. You understand that? I am begging you to stay."

"That choice was taken away from me. Just remember that I tried to break the contract. Please forgive me, Paul. This is it Paul they are boarding."

"No, Jess. I promise I will never hurt you again."

"It's not an option anymore."

"Yes, you have a choice. Don't you dare hang up that phone, Jess, or... or I will never forgive you."

She started to cry and I knew I hurt her more than I ever had in the past. I begged, "Please, Jess."

"Paul?"

"Yes."

"Please tell me you didn't mean that."

"Jess, NO! I'm desperate; please tell me where you are going? I will follow you."

I heard the dial tone. She hung up on me and left me to the empty darkness where there's no air, no light, and no Jessica. The blankness engulfed me as I gasped for air. She's gone from my life and this deep gut wrenching told me I'd never see her again.

When everything went black my body convulsed in reaction to the abandonment. A hand came around me to pull me back to reality, but I didn't want to come back without Jess. I stared into the empty space that was now my life without her. I didn't understand any of this because my world had ended. It would be easier not to live than go one day without her face to brighten my day.

# *10*

Everything left me in a daze, numb to the world. Theo's hand gripped the back of my neck as his eyes pierced into mine. His lips moved like words should be coming at me but there's nothing. Not grasping anything the air escaped my lungs while I stood there in limbo.

## *Jessica*

He would never forgive me for this. I hurt the one person that I loved more than myself. My tears continued to stream down my cheeks as I made my way down the single isle to the very last seat taking the one by the window. The idea of not seeing Paul for a full year is bad enough, but the pain in his voice told me what this did to him. Lost in my misery startled by a man standing over me when he asked, "Do you mind?"

Avoiding eye contact I nodded without looking up to show him my misery. He sat down and I heard him sniffle. A guy with a heart sitting down next to me, that's how lucky I am. He spoke to me, "What is his name?"

Not wanting to talk about my miserable life I gave him a one word answer, "Paul." My eyes wandered over to get a glimpse him. My guess is correct. He's as miserable as I am so I asked, "What is her name?"

He gave me a slight grin amongst his misery, "Alison."

Giving him an approving smile and then went back to looking out the window. The plane's engines roared and the sadness is over bearing the tears a full stream now. Leaving Paul this way had to be the worst day of my entire life.

As a gesture of comfort this guy put his hand out with his pinky in the air. Not deserving this at all I still wrapped my pinky around his. The gasp that came from him filled me with relief. We shared the same pain, the same torment, and the same comfort. We didn't need to talk to understand each other.

# Paul

Stung with a heated sensation across my face shocked me into breathing again. Tears filled my eyes when I realized Theo slapped me to my senses. Pleading with hope that he'd understand, "I love her. I kept to my promise."

He gave me a small smile while asking me, "What did she say to you before she left?"

I gasped for air, "She didn't."

Matt handed him the note. As he read it his forearm pressed against my chest holding me up against the wall. A smile grew on his face, "Paul, this tells me she loves you."

That's something I already know, "But you let her go."

"No, she tried to get out of this. She didn't want to go but she signed a contract. You understand contracts."

"No, she's gone and..." Squeezing my eyes shut, not wanting to see the reality of her loving me and then just like nothing at all she's gone from my life.

A strong sting against my face again caused the reality to come back and fill my lungs with air. Not only did I not want to come back to this nightmare I didn't want to go one day without her. Words escaped my mouth without my brain working, "shit, that hurts."

Theo laughed at me, "Are you back with us now?"

My heart bleeding, my face throbbing, and my eyes burning I nodded staring into his eyes wishing for an answer.

Theo gripped my shoulders firmly as he stated, "She wants you to wait for her if you can handle that. Boy, can you handle that?"

All I got from his determined voice is *wait for her* and *handle that.* Men aren't supposed to cry at least that's how society molds us, but losing two people I love in less than one decade. It's enough to put any man in the loony bin. So what am I supposed to do while I wait? My eyes searched Theo's eyes for answers.

The warmth of his smile, the steady gaze he gave me brought calmness to my hysteria. As if reading my mind, "Now, if you love her and you can wait for her there are things that you may want to get worked out in your life."

Lost in wonder I asked, "Like what?"

"You need to stay busy. Treat this situation like she is here at home and you just can't see her for a while."

I nodded but confused about what he said.

"You need to go back to school and finish your degree. Try to fill your days with classes, studying, and whatever else you can do to take up all your time. You don't want to ponder about where Jess is. For all you know she is at school a hundred miles from you, and she needs time to grow into a woman. Can you do this for her, for me, and for yourself, Paul? I love you like my own son and she said yes to marry you. It would be my honor to make it official. You need to handle this like a man and get your life straight."

Everything he said made sense, but cluttered into a mumble of words that rolled together. Jess is at school? Part of their family? Life straight? What is this man trying to tell me?

He turned to Matt, "I need you to make sure he does this."

Not knowing what Matt said or did because my brain numbed to the world.

Theo held my neck tighter, "How is the business, Paul?"

I shrugged, "handed it over to Tom. I wanted to be with Jess and she needed more time together."

He grinned and hugged me, "I am so happy you love my daughter." He released me and looked into my eyes, "You will handle this because she needs you in her life. Someone that cares this much about her will be rare and I believe in you."

Air entered my lungs again but the tears came to my eyes which made it impossible to see his face anymore.

Someone tossed him something but he lifted it to my face. Recognizing the softness of terrycloth I wiped my eyes so I'd see him clearly. I didn't understand why he smiled at me. It's the end of my happiness so why did he have to be happy about that.

He took a deep breath, "The house, how is it coming?"

I searched my brain for an answer, but what did this have to do with Jess? My only grasp came out, "It's not done yet."

"Well, if you two are going to get married in a year don't you suppose you should get it done?"

None of this made sense. She couldn't marry me if she's gone.

"Paul, she wants to marry you when she gets back if you will forgive her for leaving. Think about it. She didn't want to leave. She tried to get out of it. She said yes to marry you. She asked you to forgive her, and wait for her. Is that something you can do?"

I nodded as he explained this to me.

"Then you need to have a place for the both of you to live."

Finally I understood as he went over the high points. Nodding with comprehension I need him to tell me the next step.

"Go finish the school year. Go home and work on the house. Get everything in order, prepare for the future, and be ready when she comes home. I would love to see my daughter in a white gown standing next to you, son." He pulled me into the biggest bear hug, which shouldn't come from my future father in law. He took me in when no one trusted me after losing Anne.

I nodded realizing that this man has given me more support than I ever deserved and I loved him and his daughter more than my own life.

"I need you to not do anything stupid, because my daughter loves you so much that you would be cheating her of a great life with you. This is not final like Anne's death. Jessica is coming back!"

I nodded agreeing with him even though this seemed strange that he would be talking this way.

He gave me a smile and turned to Matt, "Did you get all of this, because you need to make sure he stays on track. You will call me if you need help with... call me if Paul needs help."

"Yes sir."

"I mean no time alone for a while, can you handle that?"

"Yes, sir."

"Take him back to school and make sure he stays on track. I will be up the first weekend you are at home. We will meet at the house. Paul, we are going to get started on the house."

I nodded as he let go of my neck and walked me out to the car. I got in but something didn't seem right.

Lying in my bed seemed so empty without Jess. This is the worst dream I have ever had in my life, worse than those of losing Anne. Tossing and turning couldn't push them away this horrible ache in my chest wouldn't subside. When I rolled over again I opened my eyes finding Jess there offering me comfort. Her fingers threaded through my hair relaxed me. She didn't ask me the usual question, which made things seem out of place, but she's here with me now and it's all that mattered. I pushed the painful nightmare aside when she crawled over me rubbing against me with that cute little luring smile that begged me to kiss her. Reaching up I traced my hands along her sides pulling her to me. I didn't want to hurt her or scare her off with that fear from the dream that took her away for a year. Her mouth came to mine and pressed hard and needy. She made me happy and took my breath away. She rubbed against me again and I forced myself to not close my eyes. Not wanting to get so absorbed in the moment that I might lose her. Every enticing move caused my hunger to grow. When she leaned down to nibble on my bottom lip I gave into the pleasure closing my eyes to enjoy every sensation.

Just like that she's gone. My eyes flew open in search of Jess through the emptiness that engulfed me. Reaching into the air in search of her body, and her face gasping for air as I realized I let her escape me again. I rolled over and put my face to the pillow where her head had been. The scent she left behind filled my head with her essence.

This dream came again and again, each time being a little different, but each time being more real than the last. This dream I had filled my broken heart only to have it shattered again. The hardest part was waking from it to find her gone.

I wanted to see her more so I decided to be creative. There were nights I sprinkled the drying rose petals over my bed. Other nights I lit the candles and waited for her to come to me. It's amazing to get this little time with her. To see the brightness of her eyes, the smile on her face. She's so playful and cute that I wanted to hold her forever, but every time I thought it was real I woke to her not being there.

After weeks of this I decided that I wanted to make her stay. Finding the perfect rose I went to bed with it in my hands. While I waited for her to come I planned out my persuasion to keep her here this time. It seemed like I waited forever but she did show up, only after I fell asleep. Her warmth caressed me as her hands wandered up my back massaging every tense muscle in my torso. Pleased that she made it I rolled over swiftly not only to feel her, I also needed to see her.

To my delight her grin sparkled with sin. I grabbed her thighs pulling her to me and she giggles without a sound. Confused how she could laugh without any sound worried me, but it didn't matter. She is here with me, and had every intention of keeping her. I gasped for air as I pulled her warm moist core against me again. She leaned over kissing my chest while her hips ground into my rock hard dick. The pleasure too much to endure to wait a moment longer but I had to make this last all night. Refusing to close my eyes I, willed myself to hold on to this, I bit my lip to remember the pain that would come. When she scooted down further away from me I wanted to demand that she come back here and never leave me again, but she wasn't leaving. Her hands roamed my abs, her eyes bright with mischief, and her mouth drooling, all while her intentions came clear. Her mouth dipped to the hardness she caused. Keeping my eyes on her became challenging when her tongue started at the base of my cock and trailed up to the very tip of me. I whimpered because if she put her mouth around me I wouldn't be able to hold back my release. I grabbed her wrist holding her there so she'd have to stay here with me. It's bad enough that I dreamt about her mouth wrapped around my dick but when her lips wrapped around the tip of me, not only did I close my eyes, but they rolled back in my head. Reminding myself that I shouldn't have closed my eyes I hastily opened them again searching for Jess.

My hands held only sheets, I am hard as a rock, and Jess disappeared from my life again. My glorious night with Jess had ended leaving me wanting. I got up, blew out the candles, and fell to my knees by the side of my bed. I begged god to give this one back to me. I wouldn't live through losing another love.

Night after night I prepare for my evening with Jess. I brought food one night, because if we didn't go out we would need food. Another night I stocked bottles of water. Not sure what I did wrong that made it impossible to keep her here with me? I tried everything but she wouldn't stay with me.

Matt came storming in, "That is it! I promised Mr. Jenson that I would make sure you stayed on track. You are going to class today if I have to get you in the shower myself."

He pulled me from my bed dragging me with the sheets.

"No Matt, she comes here to be with me. I need to stay here. Not sure when she is going to come back. I don't want to miss her."

"You are delusional. That is it! You are getting back to your life now. I know it's painful, but you have to be prepared. Remember what Theo said... when she comes back you'll need to be ready to marry her. If you are delusional you won't be ready."

He pulled and pushed me into the bathroom but when I flatly refused the shock of severe pain against my cheek. I grabbed my face staring at him, "What the hell did you do that for?"

"Paul, do you love her?"

"Yes, of course I do that is why I need to wait here for her to come back."

"No! Do you want her to come back?"

"Yes, but if I wait for her she comes every night. I just have to wait in the..."

"No! Is this helping you? I'll answer that. No, it's not! You need to go to school and finish the school year. We only have two and a half weeks left and you need to finish this."

I had to agree with him. I decided to get in the shower, but he continued to talk to me.

"You need to show her that you've grown up and you appreciate the time you have together, and that you will be able to support her. Besides, it doesn't help you to feel sorry for yourself."

I got out of the shower. He did leave the bathroom, but he left the door open. I walked out glaring at him, "Fine, I am going."

He grabbed his stuff and waited for me when I walked out. He laughed and I turned around in a circle wondering what he was laughing for.

"Paul, it's not final like Annie. You can change this and you have a year to get your shit together."

"Fine, I said I was going."

"Yeah, well you might want to put pants on before we go."

Taking notice that I forgot to put those on I walked back in my room and put pants on my body.

If you like the beginning of this story read It's Not Over.  You'll see what happens for Jessica and Paul once she returns home.

Other Works by Melissa M Marlow

Forever Yours (Book 1)
Wasting Away (Book 2)
Growing Tears (Book 3)
Push Away (Matters of the Heart)
Losing You (prequel to It's not Over)          ☺

Look in the future for:
It's Not Over
New Beginnings (Forever Yours Book 4)
Horse Play (Matters of the Heart)

Melissa M Marlow
www.mmmarlow.com
mmmarlow@comcast.net

www.ingramcontent.com/pod-product-compliance
Lightning Source LLC
Chambersburg PA
CBHW030557130626
46552CB00006B/2577